James Payn

Thicker than Water

Volume 3

James Payn

Thicker than Water
Volume 3

ISBN/EAN: 9783337142797

Printed in Europe, USA, Canada, Australia, Japan

Cover: Foto ©Andreas Hilbeck / pixelio.de

More available books at **www.hansebooks.com**

THICKER THAN WATER

BY

JAMES PAYN

AUTHOR OF 'BY PROXY' 'HIGH SPIRITS' ETC.

IN THREE VOLUMES

VOL. III.

LONDON

LONGMANS, GREEN, AND CO.

1883

LONDON : PRINTED BY
SPOTTISWOODE AND CO., NEW-STREET SQUARE
AND PARLIAMENT STREET

CONTENTS

OF

THE THIRD VOLUME.

CONTENTS OF THE THIRD VOLUME.

THICKER THAN WATER.

CHAPTER XXXV.

THE ROMAN VILLA.

It is a well-known though unacknowledged fact that diligent and hardworking persons can always find time for special purposes, while those who have nothing to do have rarely a moment to spare from their absorbing occupation. Thus it happened that at Letcombe Hall, whose inmates had only to follow the bent of their own fancies, arrangements for any expedition were made with difficulty, and in most cases put off indefinitely at the last moment. The treat which Professor Parks had promised himself of acting as cicerone to

Mary in the matter of the Roman Villa had
hung on hand for many weeks, and certainly
through no material obstructions. There were
vehicles in abundance at the Hall, at the disposal of any guest : the ejaculation of ' more
curricles ! ' attributed to the Indian Nabob
would have there found a ready response, but
in Mary's case not only man and horse were
needed, but a chaperon. It was impossible,
notwithstanding the eulogium passed upon the
Professor by his hostess, that he could escort
Mary alone ; the expedition was too fatiguing
for Mrs. Peyton, and the other ladies always
devised some excuse for absenting themselves.
The real reason was that they had been there
already, and suffered under the Professor's
patronage, and were not going to risk it—nay,
there was no risk, it was a certainty—to
undergo it a second time. Every one who has
visited the Royal Academy in company with
an art critic, or gone over the Docks with an
authority on statistics, will know why they
shrank from visiting the Roman Villa in

custody of Professor Parks. As a rule people
are wonderfully patient under the application
of information; a very little of it, I confess,
goes a great way with me, though I don't mind
a sprinkling; but no one likes a douche bath
of it.

It may be naturally suggested that Miss
Adela Parks was the proper person to accom-
pany her brother and Mary to this interesting
spot, and indeed this was suggested to her.
With admirable presence of mind she threw
herself upon the protection of her host.

'I correct Porson's proofs,' she said, 'but
need I listen to his lectures? Are the obliga-
tions of the tie of blood to have no limit?'
This skilful appeal to Mr. Peyton's prejudices
had the effect intended, and he threw the ægis
of his protection round her as regarded the
visit to the Roman Villa.

One morning, however, to the astonishment
of the whole party, Mr. Beryl Peyton announced his intention of going thither himself.
The revolution worked by this announcement in

the views of the Happy Family was very remarkable. It was as though Louis XIV. had,
in the depth of winter, announced his intention of going to dine in the open air at Marly.
What a moment ago would have seemed madness, became the most natural, or at all events
the most delightful, proposition in the world.
The Professor found himself for once the centre
of attraction, and was reminded by everybody
of the last (and first) time he had been so
good as to act as their cicerone. They said
that they should never forget it—which was
very true. They paid this attention to the
Professor in order that Mary should not flatter
herself that she was the cause of Mr. Peyton's
unlooked-for resolve ; but in their hearts they
knew that she *was* the cause, and that he did
not care one farthing for either the Professor's
lecture or its subject. When the vehicles
drove round to the front door, they were
found to consist of two barouches and a pony
carriage, into the latter of which, amid the
hushed amaze of all beholders, the host quietly

handed Mary Marvon and drove away with her, leaving the rest to follow, in a state of mind by no means suitable to an expedition of pleasure. The gentlemen shrugged their shoulders, the ladies looked unutterable things, and Miss Parks (who had thought it best, 'for dear Porson's sake,' to make one of the party after all) confessed to herself, with her hostess's delicate state of health in her mind, that Mr. Beryl Peyton might not after all be quite so monogamous as she had imagined.

As for Mrs. Welbeck, in replying with her laced handkerchief to a flutter of farewell from Mrs. Peyton's window, she audibly muttered, 'Poor woman!' Dr. Bilde alone wore a look of content; his habit of inflicting pain for scientific purposes, which at first had only made him indifferent, had begotten a relish for it; and the spectacle of so many fellow-creatures in the torments of jealousy, from which he himself was free, gave him a sensible satisfaction.

Though Mary Marvon was quite unaware of the envy that she had thus excited, she was conscious of the compliment her host had paid her, and, to say truth, would have gladly dispensed with it. It placed her in a position of prominence from which she shrank. But the pleasure and even triumph that had lit up Mrs. Peyton's face when she said, 'My husband intends to take you in the pony carriage,' had prevented her from showing the least unwillingness to accept his courtesy.

Beryl Peyton had an easy natural way with him, however, which put those who were themselves natural at their ease at once. Pretence was pitiful in his eyes, and flattery hateful, though his very good nature sometimes prevented its due repression. He talked of the country, its pursuits and pleasures, as compared with those of the town, and gently drew out his companion's views. Then he spoke of life at Letcombe Hall, which he said he feared was dull and gloomy to her—a question which she combated with modest gratitude, speaking, as well she might, of the kindness and consideration she had met with at Mrs. Peyton's hands, and of the deep affection which she bore her. Then he spoke of his guests, not cynically, or with the least breach of the laws of hospitality, but in a manner that astounded her, from the keen appreciation which he showed of the characters of each. She had hitherto been in doubt as to whether he was hoodwinked by them, or absolutely indifferent to their proceedings; she now found that he was neither; though their personal feelings as regarded himself seemed to have absolutely no interest for him.

'He who confers a benefit,' he said, 'and looks for gratitude, gives nothing; if he expects subservience, he sells his favours at a higher price than they are worth. It is said, Miss Marvon,' he added, with a pleasant smile, 'that the way of transgressors is hard, but I do assure you that that of the practical philanthropist is still harder.'

This was a subject on which she could be

hardly expected to have an opinion; she could only murmur something about ' deserts ' and ' merits.'

'It has of course been my object to discover them,' he replied. 'My good people '—he pointed with his thumb at the two vehicles behind them, as the proprieter of a travelling circus might have indicated the contents of his caravans—' have all something to recommend them; most of them have originality and talent, for which I can hardly be wrong in securing a fair field. But I sometimes wonder whether I am on the right tack; whether perhaps I should not do better in securing the happiness of less eminent persons. I will suppose, for argument's sake, that the worth and genuineness of each class are equal, in the latter case the benefits seem more certain, the effect more practical. What do you say, Miss Marvon?'

The question did not embarrass Mary, as perhaps he expected it would do, since he kept his eyes averted from her as he put it. It had in her eyes no personal reference to herself whatever.

'I am afraid I scarcely understand you, Mr. Peyton,' she rejoined. 'I can hardly think you can be serious——'

'I am quite serious in asking your advice,' he put in quietly.

'But if I may believe what everybody tells me, Mr. Peyton, you already practise the system of which you speak. It is not only the wise and learned, but the poor and friendless, who have reason to be grateful to you.'

'Tut, tut! that is what fools call charity; the parting with a few coppers which one doesn't want to people whose penury magnifies them to crown-pieces. The rich man who does not give to the poor is a mere chrysalis devil. No, where I have erred, as I believe, is in not having sufficiently given my attention to the well-being of young people. I should like, for example, to smooth for them the rough path of true love, and set those who are worthiest of them independent of the frowns of fate.'

'It is, at all events, a kindly aspiration,' said Mary.

'That is not very encouraging, Miss Marvon,' replied the old man, with a strange smile; 'but it is an honest answer.'

Here they arrived where the road forked. 'Would you like to see Dottrell Knob?' he said; 'it is not much out of our way.' And without waiting for her reply he took the left-hand road which led up to the downs. Here they were on a high plateau, so level that the elevation he spoke of, though of no great height, loomed before them like an Egyptian pyramid. No doubt it reminded him of this, for he presently said, 'How little can men who have not genius leave behind them to remind posterity of their existence! Their memory fades out and dwindles day by day, when once they have left the scene of their labours.'

'Fortunately, that is an idea that troubles few people,' said Mary, thoughtfully; 'at least, one's notion is that those who do most good think least about it, so far as they themselves are concerned, and thereby, without meaning it, live the longest in the hearts of others.'

'Still the hearts of others are not a very enduring sepulchre. To know that to die means to be forgotten makes death less welcome. I can remember as a young man that I thought I should never die. I seemed of such importance, not only to myself, but in the scheme of creation, that it seemed to me the very Judgment-day must needs happen first.'

Mary stared at him in wonder, not so much at the monstrous egotism of which he spoke, as at his confession of it, to a girl of her age and in her position. She did not then know that it was her companion's habit to indulge every impulse, and especially that of confiding to those who took his fancy the strangest and most secret things. Still less did she guess that this mark of favour was often the precursor to the appearance of the name of its recipient in Mr. Beryl Peyton's will.

They had now reached the Knob, a mere huge hillock of green surrounded by fir-trees, the only sign of vegetation on the whole plateau.

'It is supposed,' he said, 'though such cases of solitary sepulture are very uncommon, that one person only has been buried there, one of those early British chiefs about whom the Professor will discourse to you by the hour. I have caused, as you see—he pointed to a large fissure in the mound-side—excavations to be made in it, but they reveal nothing. When I die—or rather if I die before I have left written directions to that effect—will you be so good as to remember, Miss Marvon, that I enjoined it upon you that I should be buried there?'

Mary bowed her head; she was speechless with astonishment, and indeed with something like alarm. She called to mind what Mr. Rennie had once said of her present companion, that though some people called him a philanthropist at large, others thought he ought not to be at large, being as mad as a March hare ; and what he had just said looked really very like madness. The next moment, however, Mr. Peyton seemed to have forgotten all about his last extraordinary request, and was pointing with his whip to the spot in the valley (into which they were already descending) where lay the object of their journey.

When they reached it they found the rest of the party already arrived there, and awaiting them at the entrance of the Roman Villa ; not from respect to their host, but because the admission was sixpence a head; and they thought it just as well that that gentleman should pay it. As nothing was paid for by the guests at Letcombe Hall except their washing, the habit perhaps had become fixed, or, as they had all seen the place before and did not want to see it again, they thought it only reasonable that they should be admitted gratis. The villa had been discovered on land belonging to two small proprietors, each of whom laid claim to the exhibition of it, so that in an open turnip field there was the curious spectacle

of a couple of huts, each with a turnstile and a
money-taker, as at the Crystal Palace. Number
one claimed precedence and a superior attraction, upon the ground that what he had to
show had been first discovered ; number two
had been later in the field, but had a greater
store of antiquities to offer. So, though their
names were Brown and Jones, they had been
dubbed by the Professor, Romulus and Remus.

To my mind there is always something dis-
appointing in antiquities ; so much has to be
taken for granted, so little is visible save to the
eye of faith. Even at Pompeii one has rather
to take the word of the learned than the
evidence of one's own observation. ' This was
a public house,' for example, they tell us.
' Many dozens of amphoræ, etc. (which have
all been removed) were found here.' Of course
one doesn't expect to see the ' potboy,' nor the
inevitable hanger-on of ' pubs ' outside, waiting
for a job, but there is always a great deficiency
of detail. In this case, however, the Professor
supplied it. The first apartment in the villa,

for instance, looked uncommonly like a place
where an apartment was in course of construc-
tion, but had not as yet got beyond the ground
plan. But for the Professor, Mary would hardly
have recognised the grey marl flooring for 'tes-
seræ,' seen ' evidence of the action of fire ' in the
centre of them, or the 'five flue tiles actually
in situ.' To her uninstructed gaze they resembled
rubbish which the workmen had left and
would presently cart away. Yet there was an
earthenware drainpipe fixed into the wall, unmistakably, said the Professor, of Roman make ;
besides a heap of charcoal and some pottery,
which, though broken, was brimful of archæo-
logical interest. Then there was the hypocaust,
which, though it had tiles and a flue, was not
easy to distinguish from a neglected hothouse
wherefrom the flowerpots had been removed,
and a magnificent example (said the Professor)
of a *suspensura*, or suspended floor, though,
tired perhaps of its state of suspense, it had
vanished altogether. It is fair to state that
some apartments had really some ornamenta-

tion, though the phrase 'wall paintings of great beauty,' which the Professor applied to them, seemed a little too flattering. Among them was a faded individual with a lyre playing to various blocks and splashes in mosaic, which the Professor confidently asserted to be Orpheus and the Brutes. He insisted upon poor Mary's identifying some of these with fauns, peacocks, and the like, and on her making suggestions as to the rest. In a sort of desperation, assisted perhaps by the association of the creature with street music, she gave it as her opinion that one was a monkey, and thereby unwittingly established her reputation.

'By jingo!' exclaimed the Professor, 'and so it is; but in no Orpheus pavement, though we have many specimens of them in this favoured land, has such an animal been heretofore discovered. My dear Miss Marvon, I congratulate you; when I have finished my work on "Prehistoric Britain" I shall give my attention to these more modern matters, and you will then find yourself, I hope, not altogether unknown to fame.'

'But are you sure it *is* a monkey?' observed Mr. Nayler, cynically.

The Professor was furious ; to snatch a new discovery from the grasp of an archæologist is to rob the tigress of her last-born whelp.

'It is a presentment of one, at all events, sir,' he answered viciously.

'It is most certainly a monkey,' said Mr. Hindon, always prompt to acquiesce with the last speaker.

'And there can be no one,' sneered Dr. Bilde, who had no such instinct, 'who is a better authority on such a subject than yourself.'

If the Professor had not here interposed his authority, as being in a manner 'in the chair,' and proceeded to descant with great fire and energy upon a copper coin (looking very like a bad halfpenny) of the time of Honorius, there might have been an unpleasantness.

'What does the Professor mean?' inquired

Mary confidentially of Mrs. Welbeck, 'by a coin being found *in situ?* '

'Heaven knows, my dear,' answered that lady, who did not quite perceive the point of the observation, 'but I saw him take it out of his pocket.'

Up to this point Mary had earned 'golden opinions from the lecturer by reason of her attention and intelligence; but her reputation was doomed to be shortlived. They had now arrived in the Chamber of the Four Seasons; that is, the chamber whose floor had in each of its four corners a representation of the seasons, but only one was left. It depicted a lady with very scanty drapery, and the great question was, Was she Summer or was she Winter? It was argued, with what might be literally termed a decent probability, that nothing but a very high temperature could have excused her appearing in so very slight a garb; she had, however, an object in her hand which some persons of imagination, among whom was the Professor, contended was a starved bird, and on the strength of this allegorical design they insisted upon it that she was Winter. The Professor had just opened his brief upon this favourite subject, which naturally required delicate and euphemistic treatment, when a terrible thing happened to Mary: she heard in the next apartment her host speaking to some newcomer in a tone of hearty welcome, and then a reply in tones that had once been dear to her, but which she had hoped never to hear again.

'You were quite right to come on here,' said Mr. Peyton, cheerily. 'I owe you an apology for not remaining at home to receive you.' Then came the voice again, uttering some commonplace courtesy, which nevertheless set poor Mary's heart beating and her pretty cheeks aflame. Of the Professor's lecture she caught nothing: she knew that he was appealing to her about the starved bird, but did not know that he was calling the opponents of his theory hard names; she only caught the one word parrot.

'Yes,' she said, with a pretence of earnest conviction, 'no doubt it's a parrot.'

There was a little shout of laughter, in which the Professor did not join, a sudden silence such as is caused by a new arrival, and then his introduction to the various members of the party by his host. Mary did not turn her eyes that way, but kept them fixed upon the starved bird till Mr. Peyton's voice addressed her.

'Miss Marvon, my friend Mr. Edgar Dornay—one of the young people,' he added in a whisper, 'I have asked to Letcombe, in hopes to make the Hall more pleasant to you.'

CHAPTER XXXVI.

DISCORDANT ELEMENTS.

How much more happiness there would be in the world if only people were allowed to be happy in their own way! But even the best of men and women, who really have at heart the happiness of others, too often disregard this; they insist upon making people happy *their* way, and fail egregiously.

Jones loves Smith, and Jones loves Brown, but, not content with their reciprocation of his affection, he wants Smith and Brown to be devoted to each other. This, however, they steadily refuse to be: Smith cannot imagine what Jones sees in Brown, and Brown cannot imagine what Jones sees in Smith, and when it is pointed out to them they deny its existence.

A very strong Jones might take Smith and
Brown and knock their heads together, but to
unite their hearts he will find impossible;
and, if this coalition be difficult in matters of
friendship, how much more so is it in those of
love!

It was one of the weaknesses of Mr. Beryl
Peyton to be blind to this fact. He was mas-
terful by nature; wealth and power had increased this characteristic in him; and when
he said 'Bless you, my children, love one
another,' to two young people, he expected
them to do it and not to be long about it
either.

He had conceived a great regard, as we
know, for Mary Marvon, and, thinking in his
princely manner over what he could do for her,
it struck him that he would make an heiress of
her and marry her to Mr. Edgar Dornay. He
had taken a fancy to Edgar, as being a young
man of intelligence and position who took an
interest in the affairs of other people; and,
though development of artistic taste in the

middle classes did not seem to Mr. Peyton so vital as it does to some people (for apart from his own particular weaknesses he was a man of sense), he admitted there was something in it, and at all events was pleased to see one of our golden or gilt youths, the young gentleman in question, concerning himself with that question instead of devoting himself exclusively to the ballet and pigeon-shooting.

Of Mary's former acquaintance with Edgar he had no suspicion, though, if he had taken the trouble to reflect upon it, he would have seen the probability of it. It was a subject on which Mrs. Peyton had her reasons for silence; and indeed in any case she would not have ventured to trouble her husband with any such matter, which he would have set down under the general head of ' rubbish ' or ' tittle-tattle.' He had, indeed, casually informed her that he meant to invite Mr. Ralph Dornay and his newly married wife to Letcombe Dottrell—an intention, as we know, she had communicated to Mary—but he had not said one word about

Edgar. Nay, what was curious, when one remembers his views upon the tie of blood, he had never asked himself the question whether Ralph's society would be agreeable to his nephew, or *vice versâ*.

Under the circumstances one can imagine what a charming addition to the Happy Family —their relations to one another being such as have been described—these three new-comers, with *their* relations to one another, must needs have been. That Charles Sotheran, no friend of Edgar's, and an open foe of Ralph's, should have also arrived on the same day, would in itself have been an embarrassing circumstance, but for the other entanglements and dilemmas, which by contrast made that smooth sailing, and threw its awkwardness into the shade. It would have been only natural for Charley to have put up at Bank Cottage; but Mr. Peyton, in pursuance of his notable plan of making the Hall pleasant to Mary, had insisted on his being his guest; and it is fair to say that in this he was not depriving Mrs. Sotheran of her son's society, since he had obtained from the authorities of the Probate Office a special holiday for Charley, independent of his usual vacation.

In the Roman Villa Edgar and Mary had met as strangers : the former, whatever his faults, was a gentleman after all—albeit of the superficial sort—and, perceiving her distress and embarrassment, had confined himself to the coldest civilities. He, of course, had been aware that he should meet her at Letcombe Hall, and perhaps had entertained a hope that he had been invited thither not without her cognisance, or even approval ; if it was so, her manner had disabused him of that idea at once. He felt that he had no chance with her, that his appearance had pained and annoyed her exceedingly, and, to do him justice, he had henceforth no other object than to make his stay under the same roof as little embarrassing to her as possible. Mr. Peyton, like the rest, had taken them for strangers to one another, and in driving home with Mary had spoken to

her of Edgar under that misapprehension. She
was thereupon compelled to tell him that they
had known one another before, but did not feel
called upon to say under what circumstances.
She could not conceal a certain awkwardness in
speaking of the matter, and this he set down to
a cause the exact contrary to that from which
it arose. He fancied that she was not indifferent to Edgar, and that she had purposely
adopted an airy manner towards him to conceal
the fact, not only from others but himself; it
might easily have happened that the difference
in their positions as to means had hitherto
placed, and still seemed to place, an insuperable
bar between them ; and hence her unwillingness to encourage him—an idea which, as often
happens, fitted in with the wishes and intentions of him who entertained it. It was one
of Mr. Beyrl Peyton's favourite occupations
to remove insuperable bars. He presently
informed Mary that Ralph Dornay and his
wife were coming to the Hall that very
day.

'The raptures of the honeymoon,' he added with a grim smile, 'are not, I suppose, quite over, so they have preferred to travel by themselves rather than in the same train with Edgar.'

Mary thought to herself that there might have been other reasons, and even that if they knew he had been invited they would not have come at all.

In this, however, she was mistaken. Things had happened since she had parted from Mrs. Beckett of which she knew nothing; and a reconciliation of a somewhat skin-deep kind had taken place. That a change had come over Lady Orr (as she now termed herself) was evident enough; she was standing with Mrs. Peyton at the front door as the pony carriage drew up, and hardly waiting for the expression of her host's welcome, not only held out both her hands to Mary, but, encouraged doubtless by her forgiving face, drew her towards her in an affectionate embrace.

'Let bygones be bygones, my dear,' she whispered ; and, as Mary kissed her, she felt the other's tears upon her cheek.

'What *can* have happened?' thought Mary ; but she was well pleased at what had come of it, whatever it was. She was human enough in her resentment of wrong and insult, but at the least show of penitence—and this was something more, it was tender remorse— her heart melted like wax. For the moment, however, she attributed Mrs. Beckett's behaviour, in part at least, to Mrs. Peyton's influence, who was looking on at this little scene with obvious satisfaction.

In the great hall they found Mr. Ralph Dornay, examining the pictures on the walls with a critical eye. His reception by Mr. Peyton (who had never seen him before) was sufficiently cordial, but by no means the same welcome he had given to his wife. His manner, though singularly courteous (when he did not intend it to be otherwise), could boast of many gradations. Ralph seemed to feel that there

was leeway to be made up, and was so profuse
in his compliments and his self-congratulations
at finding himself at Letcombe Dottrell that he
seemed to forget Mary's presence altogether,
till his host drew his attention to it.

'Miss Marvon I think you know.'

'I have that honour,' said Ralph, with a
beaming smile, and touched Mary's hand with
his finger-tips.

He saw at once that she was in favour, and
that the scornful patronage with which he had
intended to treat her would be very injudicious; on the other hand, he knew her character too well to expect any advantage from
conciliation. To have gained a footing at
Letcombe Hall, even as Lady Orr's husband,
was a great step for Mr. Ralph Dornay; and it
was an object with him to make it secure. He
had views altogether different from those he had
entertained in his bachelor days; and in the
greeting which he presently gave to his nephew,
though studiously polite, it was easy to see that
the countenance of the 'head of the house'

was no longer of much consequence to him.
He had found his present pecuniary position a
much better passport to society, though somewhat irregularly used, than the blood of the
Dornays. 'Openings in life' are not for young
men only; middle age has also its aspirations;
and Ralph had in his eye, not only a 'position
in the county,' where his wife's country house
was situated, but a seat in Parliament. His
deportment had been always unexceptionable;
but he now began to use a certain dignity,
especially to those he considered his inferiors.
When Charley Sotheran, for example, made his
appearance at the Hall just before the dinner-
hour (having dutifully passed his afternoon at
Bank Cottage), Ralph Dornay acknowledged his
somewhat cool 'How are you?' with stately
frigidity, and pushed out two fingers, as though
they had been the antennæ of an insect, by way
of salutation; whereupon Charley also pushed
out two, so that, instead of shaking hands, these
gentlemen appeared to be crossing swords with

their fingers—an action, as it turned out, which might have been taken as very significant of their mutual relations.

Of this last meeting Mary was not a spectator. She had been glad enough to go to her own room and stay there in quiet after the occurrences of the day. She had not been long occupied with her own reflections when Mrs. Peyton knocked at her sitting-room door. ‘The house is now so full of people, my dear,’ she said apologetically, ‘that I must snatch a quarter of an hour with you when I can. How did you like the Roman Villa, or rather the Professor’s dissertation upon it? I am afraid you have had more than enough of it.’

‘I confess, dear Mrs. Peyton, that I am a little tired.’

‘There was something else to trouble you besides the lecture, was there not, my dear?’ continued the old lady, very tenderly. ‘When we were talking of a certain person the other day, I little dreamt that we should see him here : indeed, as you know, I was ignorant of his identity. You may be quite certain it is not my fault——’

‘My dear Mrs. Peyton, it was nobody’s fault,’ put in Mary. Then with a smile, which to say the truth was a little forced, she added, ‘ Nay, it is not even any one’s misfortune. As I told you the other day, I have got over that matter: it is almost as though it had never been.’

‘You say “ almost,” Mary ; now pray tell me—for indeed I do not ask it without reason —what you mean by that word.’

‘I mean that though I can never love Edgar Dornay again, the sight of him did give me some distress ; for a day or two it may still continue to do so ; but—I am sure of this from what I feel already—his presence will affect me less and less. Of course,’ she added, ‘ if I thought he had come down here with any idea of pressing his attentions on me, why then I should go away.’

‘Go away ! Good heavens, do not talk like that ! ’ exclaimed Mrs. Peyton, with alarm.

'You do not know what that would mean to me, my darling. Of course he shall not press them. I only wanted to make certain of your own sentiments.'

'They are as fixed as fate and quite unalterable,' said Mary, with a touch of haughtiness. 'On the other hand, I must needs absolve Mr. Dornay, so far as I could judge by his manner, of any intention of annoying me.'

'No doubt, no doubt,' said the old lady, thoughtfully. 'I feel sure he comes here with no such intention : it was not his doing at all. You must not mind if you are placed next to him at dinner. I will let him know that it is not your wish.'

'That will be quite unnecessary,' said Mary, drawing herself up and speaking very coldly. 'Forgive me, dear Mrs. Peyton,' she added tenderly, perceiving distress in the other's looks ; 'I know I have no right to be proud, but a girl's love—whoever she be—is her own to give or to withhold.'

'Quite true, quite true,' assented the old lady.

'Would that all girls were like you!' Then men, perhaps,' she added with a sigh, 'would be less sinful. All I wish to say is, that if Edgar Dornay seems to be thrown in your way here it will not be his doing.'

'Thrown in my way!' echoed Mary, in amazement.

'Yes; it may be so just for a little while. If it is so, do not visit it upon him as if it were his fault. Bear with it, darling, for my sake. Oh! why did they come, why did they come, to vex you when we were so happy?'

'Dear Mrs. Peyton, do not weep,' said Mary, throwing herself upon her knees and kissing the old lady's hands; 'who am I that a little inconvenience to me—for that is what it all comes to, after all—should thus affect you? Why should we not be as we were before? How long are they going to stay?'

'I don't know, darling. I know nothing. Perhaps for a week or two; perhaps—but it is impossible to say; people come here for a week and stay for years. Some one will come some

day and take you away from me. Or perhaps
I shall die and leave you to their tender
mercies. Oh! Mary, darling, if I could only
see you married to the man of your choice!'

'But I don't want to be married,' said Mary,
laughing ; ' and I haven't made a choice.'

'Hush!' cried Mrs. Peyton; ' what is
that?'

Through the evening air there rang out the
cheerful notes of a key bugle. Some one was
playing it on the verandah that ran round the
house; and it seemed to awaken the echoes
from a hundred hills.

'I—I think,' said Mary, ' it must be
Charley ; at least I know that he does play the
bugle, and that the Echo Song is his delight ;
but he would surely never venture——'

'Hark, hark !' murmured Mrs. Peyton; ' it
is my Henry's bugle. Dear, dear, if Beryl
were to hear it!'

If Beryl did not hear it, Beryl must have
been as deaf as Marcom, his mute. The key
bugle, played however skilfully, is scarcely

muffled music. There is small dispute as to its
being the most inspiriting of instruments. Even
Mrs. Peyton, despite the melancholy association to which she had alluded, felt a sense of
cheeriness, as she listened to it, to which she
had been a stranger for many a year. As for
Mary, the melody stirred her heart within her,
and seemed, like a wholesome breeze, to sweep
away the atmosphere of intrigue and greed
that permeated Letcombe Hall.

'I suppose that confounded row means
dinner in half an hour,' ejaculated Ralph
Dornay, who had already retired to his dress-
ing-room; for his toilette, always elaborate,
now consumed more time than ever.

But the music meant nothing of the sort;
it was simply a happy thought of Charley's,
who, having been informed by the garrulous
Mrs. Welbeck of the existence of his favourite instrument somewhere in the house, had
ferreted it out at her request, and, without
leave or licence, was exercising its vocal
powers.

The Happy Family were astonished, but by no means displeased: they foresaw that in taking this unprecedented liberty one of the new-comers had done for himself in the eyes of their host and patron. Had they known that this particular sound was connected with the habits of his dead son, they would have been jubilant indeed, since they would have felt certain of its arousing his extreme resentment; but noise of all kinds they knew he hated, and confidently calculated upon an outburst of indignation.

As Mary left her room she met Mr. Peyton in the passage, and they descended the great stairs together.

'What charming airs some one has been playing on the bugle!' she said.

'Do you think so?' he answered quickly. 'I am sure it will please the player to hear it.'

Mary blushed at this; perhaps for shame at having spoken of Charley's performance so diplomatically.

Mr. Peyton looked at her with a pleased

smile. 'Such a burst of melody was a little alarming,' he said; 'but, as you say, it was very exhilarating. It is like the breath of youth, and puts new life in this old house. I knew Dornay was musical, but I had no idea he played the bugle.'

Mary was silent, and, feeling that her silence was almost an act of duplicity, blushed again.

Nothing more was said on the subject until they were seated at dinner, to which Edgar took her in at Mrs. Peyton's request. Then the host, looking across the table to the young couple, observed in a loud voice, 'Your performance in the verandah just now was much admired, let me tell you, Dornay, by your fair neighbour.'

Edgar looked up in some surprise. 'It was not I, sir, I assure you; I have not the skill, nor even the breath for it.'

'Then who on earth was it?' asked Mr. Peyton, knitting his brow.

'If you mean the key bugle and that row

in the verandah, sir,' said Charley, modestly, 'I am afraid that was me.'

Then followed an uncomfortable silence, broken only by Mr. Hindon's sympathetic tones.

'A very candid confession, Mr. Sotheran, though not quite grammatically expressed. Your frankness does you honour.'

CHAPTER XXXVII.

DR. BILDE.

As regarded the new arrivals at the Hall, and
the effects produced by them upon the Happy
Family, the result of the first day's innings—
and even of the next two or three—was dis-
tinctly in favour of Charles Sotheran.   It was
easily to be seen that Edgar Dornay, and not
he, was first favourite with Mr. Beryl Peyton ;
and to be not a favourite, and still more to be
' out of the running,' was equivalent to popu-
larity with this very peculiar ' ring.'   As Mr.
Peyton, however, was not actually hostile to
Charley, but only discouraging, some thought
it worth their while to play him against Edgar,
and to make friends with him on their own
account.   His natural and outspoken ways,

so different from the manner that they would themselves have assumed had they been in his position, gave them the impression of simplicity, and seemed to adapt him for a catspaw. They took his satire, which was sometimes sufficiently severe, for awkwardness, and imagined, even while they winced, that he trod upon their toes by mistake, and not by design. To them Edgar's cultivated tone and greater knowledge of the world made him appear, even without his host's obvious goodwill, a much more formidable rival.

Mr. Marks, indeed, who had a natural turn for intrigue, and thought he detected in Mary's manner a leaning towards Charley, determined to use this guileless young Government clerk for his own purposes, and laid himself out to please him ; and what greater benefit (thought he) could he confer upon him than to teach him the science of metaphysics? He therefore took him out—as a philosopher of old might have taken some promising youth into the groves of Academe—into the woods and fields, and discoursed of ' Kant's method,' to Charley's obvious enjoyment. It was a stroke of humour, as the young man well understood, of which Fortune could not have many samples in her bag, and he welcomed it accordingly. There was a terrace-walk within view, but out of earshot of the house, which was Mr. Marks's favourite training ground. Let us listen as they discourse together; one great advantage in metaphysics being, that one can strike in anywhere and understand from an isolated fragment as much as may be gathered from an entire system.

'But where are our Categories?' inquires Mr. Marks; 'the rules which the Understanding, by means of its own essential law, lays at the foundation of Nature for joining all the given Divinity in our consciousness—do you follow me, Mr. Sotheran?'

Charley nodded. As he certainly did not keep up with Mr. Marks, it was allowable, perhaps, thus to indicate that he followed him.

'It would be difficult, you see, my young friend, to get on without the Categories.'

'Very difficult,' admitted Charley, whose head was revolving.

'Moreover, our Category extends beyond the Sensible.'

'Most certainly,' said Charley, eagerly. Whenever he could conscientiously agree with Mr. Marks, he did it with effusion.

'The fact is, if I take away all thinking (in other words, what occurs through the Categories) from an empiric cognition, there remains no cognition at all, since by mere intuition nothing at all is thought. Then, what is the question that presents itself?'

As the speaker here hovered over his subject, Charley imagined that he was being interrogated. 'Why think at all?' he hazarded.

For a moment Mr. Marks regarded him with severe suspicion ; but, perceiving in the young man's face an earnest gravity (the same he wore when interviewed by legatees in the Probate Office), he answered, 'There is something in that; the conception of a Noumenon.'

'I hope so,' said Charley, modestly; 'but I am not absolutely certain of what a Noumenon is.'

'Well, it's a long story,' said Mr. Marks. 'A Noumenon, however, to state it briefly, is the opposite of a phenomenon. That gentleman yonder'—he indicated Mr. Josiah Nayler, who was approaching them with the object of breaking up their conference—'is a Noumenon.'

Mr. Nayler was jealous of the attraction which Mr. Marks's conversation seemed to have for Charley, and would fain have taught him his great system of the unsubstantiality of things. But, unfortunately for his hopes of a proselyte, he had offended Charley. After his rejection by Mary Marvon, Mr. Nayler had begun perhaps to have doubts as to whether that young lady was not a presentment after all; at all events he treated her as if she had no existence. To say that Charley resented this was much to understate his indignation. There were occasions (such as when Mr. Nayler would ignore some remark of Mary's, or lift his eyes in scornful indifference of it) when Charley could hardly help 'going for' the legs of that lofty philosopher, for higher he could not have hit him. In any other way than by doing battle against Mary's enemies, poor Charley could not show his devotion. Not only did she herself offer him no encouragement, but Mrs. Peyton had privately informed him that to pay that young lady any marked attention would injure her in the estimation of her host. She even went so far as to hint to him that her husband had set his heart upon an alliance between her and Mr. Edgar Dornay—an idea that would have been insupportable to him, had he not been well persuaded that such an event could never take place. Indeed, it was not desired even by Edgar himself. 'First love,' he openly observed in his light way, 'is like a half-smoked cigar: when once it has gone out the aroma is fled; it will never take the match again; there is nothing for it but to try another weed.'

Dr. Bilde nodded assent, but disbelieved the speaker. His keen eye had detected that previous relations of a confidential kind had at one time existed between Edgar and Mary, and, judging from his own resolute soul, deemed passion to be less evanescent. He concluded that, if Edgar had given up hope, jealousy of a successful rival would at least remain with him, and calculated upon his hostility to Charley, and on his readiness to do him an ill turn. The Doctor alone of all the Happy Family had recognised in the young Government clerk, not only an uncompromising antagonist, but a foe-man worthy of his steel; but he was not on that account made more particular as to his weapons—the very last thing he thought of was a fair fight.

It must not be supposed that Charley's free and easy manner towards him, or even the scornful way with which he ventured to combat his most cherished theories, were alone the cause of his enmity. There was a far deeper reason for it; so deep that none but himself ever guessed at its existence. He hated the young fellow because he perceived that he loved Mary, and suspected her of reciprocating his love—for Dr. Bilde intended Mary for himself.

It was true he despised her opinions, which in her mouth made him furious. Her kindness of heart, her gentleness to all about her, were not only lost upon him, but even exercised such an attraction of repulsion that he was capable, if he had dared, of using the most offensive language to her. It could not quite be said of him—

> He hated her with the hate of Hell,
> But loved her beauty passing well;

for his nature was rather cold than gross, but his dislike of the best qualities of her heart and mind were overpowered by his admiration for her as a woman. Her independence of character and obvious indifference to her own interests, as regarded Mr. Peyton, exacted his unstinted homage ; and he felt that, if he could only win her, she could be made a worthy mate for him. He looked upon her with the eyes of an ornamental gardener, who sees immense capabilities in a landscape when certain objectionable features shall have been carted away. Yet his spirit was so proud and unbending that he could never swallow a single prejudice, or bate one jot of a dogma, however objectionable in her sight, to recommend himself to her. One may be allowed to imagine (though the idea never so much as crossed Mary's mind), being such as he was as a lover, what sort of a husband this cast-iron man was likely to make.

In her presence he never stooped to pretence, lest (looking, as his custom was, into the future) he should one day give her an opportunity of humiliating him ; but with others, in order to obtain her, he had no such scruples. I am afraid it even now suggested itself to him that at no far distant time he would be in a position to make her pay for her audacity in opposing herself to him.

It was necessary to the success of his plans to make friends with Edgar Dornay; and this was not achieved without eating a leek or two, and the Doctor did not like leeks. Like many other young gentlemen, nowadays, who have nothing to do, Edgar was 'devoted' to Art, and flirted with what he had the impudence to call her 'handmaid' Poetry. Indeed, within the last few weeks he had published a volume of poems, 'Heart Throbs,' which had made some noise in the world; the little world, that is, in which he lived, for as to the general public they paid no more attention to it than a man who has no intention of travelling pays to the thud of a fog-signal. The book was full of harmonious echoes, the only exception being a vehement lyrical attack upon the faithlessness of the fair sex, evoked by that double rejection with which we are acquainted, and really containing some original and vigorous lines. To those who knew the circumstances which occasioned it, it also showed great powers of the imagination, for the poet represented himself as not only being in no wise to blame in the matter in question, but as having been treated with much cruelty and deception. This book Dr. Bilde, by an immense effort of intellectual self-denial, and by sitting, as it were, upon all the safety-valves of natural expression, actually brought himself to praise, and thereby made a short cut into its author's good graces.

By this means he put himself on friendly terms with Edgar, and in the combat between himself and Charley, which not seldom enlivened the dinner-table, at least secured his neutrality. The war was not only to the knife between them, but generally about the knife: experiments, and especially vivisection, were the Doctor's hobby; nor, although he knew that not only Mary herself, but Beryl Peyton, regarded his views on these matters with little short of loathing, could he restrain the expression of them or conceal his contempt for all objectors. The simplest observation from the most ignorant inquirer was sufficient to set him going; nor, with all his wits, had he the power to discriminate questions which were put to him in good faith from those suggested, as they often were by Charles Sotheran, for the purpose of drawing him out and exposing his natural callousness of heart.

'Pain,' he would say, 'was nothing as compared with the acquisition of knowledge.'

'You mean the pain inflicted upon others is nothing,' Charley would reply, 'as compared with knowledge acquired by oneself.'

And then there would ensue a contest so bitter that presently Mr. Beryl Peyton would himself have to interfere to stop it, just as in the lists of old the king would cast down his royal *bâton* to prevent contest becoming carnage. I am afraid Mr. Peyton took some pleasure in these jousts, and I am sure Charley did.

'I like to bait the brute,' he once confessed to Lady Orr, who was remonstrating with him upon the subject: 'only think how he must have baited other brutes!'

And Lady Orr, who was always pictur-
ing to herself her magnificent Alexander
pegged down to a table, and slowly done to
death by this scientific miscreant, admitted
that he deserved all he got. If the Doctor
had but known when to hold his tongue, he
could, logically, have broken Charley across
his knee; but, as it was, he was like some
enormous whale spouting angry foam attacked
by a small but agile swordfish.

Once he had a bad toothache, which did
not tend to soothe him. In answer to kind
inquiries, he observed that he had discovered
an abscess.

'Then you must be all right,' said Charley.
'Pain is nothing as compared with the acquisition of knowledge.'

At this Dr. Bilde forgot to maintain that
'scientific attitude' which he was always
recommending as the proper one for all persons of sense; in vulgar phrase, he lost his
temper.

'My dear sir,' argued Charley, 'you tell us

" tenderness of feeling is a proof of intellectual weakness," and therefore I should be a fool to pity you.'

It was a favourite pastime with this young gentleman to egg on Mrs. Welbeck, who, though in reality she talked for the sake of talking, professed to be very desirous of information, to ask the most absurd questions of the Doctor, which, nevertheless, since they were in connection with his hobby, obtained attention and a reply.

For example : 'I do hope, Dr. Bilde,' she observes one day, in her artless manner, 'that you have never vivisected a cat.'

' I have vivisected fifty cats, madam.'

'Dear, dear, how shocking! and I am so fond of cats.'

' At all events, let me assure you that I am not fond of vivisecting them. They scratch and squeal so, that I had rather operate on any other animal.'

At this there is a horrible silence, of the cause of which Dr. Bilde is profoundly ignorant, and to which, if he had understood it, he would have been profoundly indifferent.

'Then as to the poor dogs,' continues Mrs. Welbeck, proceeding with her investigations, ' do they not bark and bite ? '

'They do in Watts's hymns,' returns the Doctor, grimly, ' but not on the dissecting table ; indeed, as to barking, we take care to stop that ; operators who know their business always make a point of dividing the laryngeal nerve as a preliminary.'

'Poor Alexander !' murmurs Lady Orr. 'My prayer would be, if Dr. Bilde ever got hold of him, that he should go mad and bite him.'

The disgust and loathing expressed in Mary's face are unmistakable ; there is a heavy frown on Beryl Peyton's brow ; but Dr. Bilde, true to his principles, scorns to express one syllable of extenuation or regret. The bull excited by the banderillos is becoming ripe for the toreador.

' Useful as these little experiments on animals may be, Dr. Bilde,' observes Charley, with the air of a scientific inquirer, ' I suppose if practised on human beings they would have infinitely more significance.'

' No doubt, no doubt, sir,' admits the Doctor, deceived by the other's tone. ' There is so much prejudice, however, abroad—or rather at home, for things in France look much more hopeful—that one despairs of science having fair play.'

' How about criminals ? ' suggests Charley.

At this fancy fly the trout rises with vivacity.

' A very sensible idea, young gentleman, which has, however, occurred to others. What possible objections, save such as occur to folks who have poached eggs for brains, can be urged against thus utilising condemned persons, for the benefit of the world they are about to leave? It is a plan that recommends itself to every true thinker. On the other hand, there is that troublesome question of relatives ' (here he looked towards the host, as being certain of his sympathy in that branch of his argument at all events). 'Parents especially are sure to make a commotion.'

'How about pauper children who are orphans, about whom no stir is likely to be made?' inquires Charley.

Dr. Bilde is about to remark that public opinion is not yet ripe for the 'utilisation' of orphan children, when he catches Edgar Dornay's eye. That gentleman has far too delicate a taste to sympathise with brutality, even under the guise of science, but he does not approve of a man who can appreciate 'Heart Throbs' being turned into ridicule. Dr. Bilde, thanks to his warning look, suddenly discovers that Charley has been drawing him out, and the entertainment is concluded for that day.

But though Dr. Bilde had conciliated Edgar Dornay, he could not persuade him to join him in alliance offensive and defensive against the man he took for granted was their common enemy. Edgar had no liking for Charley, but he had no animosity against him ; nor, although

Dr. Bilde took infinite pains to delicately imply that he was in fact his successful rival, could he be moved to aggression. Without having any claim to be called chivalrous, the fact was that Edgar had—up to a certain point—the feelings of a gentleman, which in Dr. Bilde's case did not rise over his shoes. Born of ' poor but honest ' parents, the Doctor had carried out the usual programme of the self-made man of the intellectual type. If money-making had been his aim in life, he would of course have come to town with half a crown in his pocket, and swept out a shop; but he had remained in his native village and devoted himself to study. It was a favourite boast with him that he had learnt to write, in order to save paper, on the polished thigh-bone of a horse (which Charley used to suggest he had previously vivisected); and, in an education conducted on such an economical scale, it is probable that the proverbial extra twopence for manners had never been paid. At all events he had none; and, being naturally devoid of feeling, ' the instinct of a gentleman,' which is sometimes, though very rarely, found in mannerless men, was wholly wanting in him. Nor could he understand its existence in others. Having discovered, for certain, that for some reason (to him inscrutable) Edgar Dornay would be no party to a certain scheme of ' Thorough ' which he had resolved to put in practice against Charley, he looked about him for another ally ; and, somewhat to his surprise, found one very ready to his hand.

CHAPTER XXXVIII.

AN EAVESDROPPER.

A COUP D'ÉTAT, even though it may have the completest success, has almost always some unpleasant consequences ; it can never compare with the gradual advances made by good sense towards good government; and this truth in politics holds good in social life. By one bold push Ralph Dornay had found his way through insurmountable obstacles to the very height of fortune, had gained a position which even in his audacious youth had never entered into his dreams, but yet he was not happy. But there are always inconveniences in sitting on a pinnacle, and in his case they were increased by the consciousness of how he got there. If one might venture on such a comparison in the case of a gentleman who was practically in the enjoyment of 30,000*l.* a year, he was like a person who, having committed by a happy impulse a most successful murder, has made no arrangements for concealing the evidences of his crime. His capture of the rich widow was so suddenly conceived, and so promptly carried out, that he had not had time to give due consideration to his subsequent behaviour. He knew, of course, that she had married him out of pique, but, if he had been a wise·man, he would never have let her know that he knew it. He might not have been able to convince her of his own disinterested love, but to hint that so far as that question was concerned he and she were quits was most injudicious; yet on their first quarrel, which had taken place within twenty-four hours of their wedding, he had more than hinted as much. A woman of sense will bear a good deal from a bad husband, but she will not stand being reminded of her own folly in having married him.

Of course, their quarrel was about money

matters. Mr. Rennie had carried out the widow's directions to the letter in tying up her property, and even her income was supposed to be at her own disposal; but in this latter matter the law lends itself to an agreeable fiction. It places the money, indeed, in the wife's hand; but the husband, being the stronger, forces her fingers open with a gentle violence, and puts it into his own pocket. The phrase 'for her separate use and maintenance' becomes in short synonymous with 'robbery from the person,' and there is no remedy. Ralph Dornay wore a velvet glove upon his iron hand; his touch was gentle, but his grasp was full of power. It was in accordance with his own interests—that is, with his ambition to take a high place in society—to behave with propriety to his wife, and he showed her every external mark of respect; but at a very early date he had decided—shortly and sharply too—the great matrimonial question of Who shall be master? in his own favour. It is not too much to say that from that moment his wife detested him. When she looked in her looking-glass she said to herself 'Fool!' but when she looked at him (which was more seldom) she said to herself 'Thief!' Outwardly they were a well-behaved couple enough; one would have concluded, perhaps, from their mutual behaviour, that their marriage had been one of 'convenience': but, as Edgar observed of them, 'one would not have guessed that the convenience had been so entirely on one side.'

Except for that bitter speech, Edgar said little against his uncle, though he probably made up for that by thinking. He had, as we know, been in a manner reconciled to him: this had been brought about by Lady Orr. Her husband had insisted on it, but we may be sure she made no mention of that to his nephew. She had written to Edgar requesting an interview, and he had called upon her in Park Lane. The bride had met him very frankly, except that she dropped no syllable of that relation to him which had at one time been 'on the cards,' and had thrown herself upon his generosity.

'There is nothing you can tell me,' she said, 'of the ill behaviour of my husband towards yourself, which I cannot guess. What I am about to ask of you is for my own sake, not for his. *You* will not humiliate me, I am sure.'

This last phrase, while on the one hand it revealed everything, presented the whole question in a nutshell. Edgar bit his lips, but bowed in acquiescence.

'I know it,' she said ; 'whatever has been amiss with you, *you* are a gentleman. Unfortunate as my position is, through my own fault——'

He waved his hand just a little, for which she was very grateful ; she knew he meant to signify that the fault was not all her own.

'It will be made ten times more unfortunate should you stand aloof from us. You know what the world is saying even as it is.'

'I do not wish to stand aloof from you, Lady Orr.'

'It is of my husband that I speak ; you,

Edgar, are his nephew, his only relative, and the head of his family. If you refuse to take his hand because he has given it to me, it is I who shall be the sufferer.'

'Madam,' he said, 'my uncle is a scoundrel.'

She looked neither shocked nor pained, but smiled a bitter smile that went to his very heart. If she had said, 'Great heavens, do you suppose I have not found that out for myself?' her lips could not have spoken it more plainly than that smile did. 'It is for my sake,' she murmured.

Edgar Dornay was not a Dr. Bilde: he had a heart which would have melted at any woman's tears, and this woman had been kind and dear to him. So for her sake he had taken his uncle's hand, and there was peace between them. Ralph did not trouble himself to inquire how the reconciliation had been brought about; he thought that Edgar had shown his wisdom in not 'quarrelling with his bread and butter,' and accepted the result without much thankfulness. The countenance of the head of his house was, as we have said, not of the same importance to him as it had been; but still it *was* important, and, now that he found himself under the same roof with Edgar, it was a matter of considerable satisfaction to him that matters had been made smooth between them.

Ralph's relations with Mr. Charles Sotheran had seemed to him by comparison of small consequence; but as the days went on at Letcombe Hall he altered his views on that matter. It was plain that Mary Marvon was the reigning favourite with both her host and hostess, and it was no less plain that Charley was in love with Mary. Charley, it seemed, was not so popular with Mr. Beryl Peyton as Edgar was; it was even clear to Ralph's keen eye that the old man was planning a match between the latter and Mary—an arrangement that would have been distasteful to Ralph, considering the state of that young lady's feelings towards himself. He knew enough of her, it is true, to be sure that it would never take place ; but in the meantime, and so long as a chance remained of her complying with Mr. Peyton's wishes, Mary was all-powerful. Nay, it was not certain, even if she went counter to them and accepted Charley, that she would altogether lose her hold on the old man's affections.

The very idea of this—that the girl who despised him should marry the young fellow he detested, and be prosperous into the bargain—was wormwood. None who knew Ralph Dornay—or who knew, as we do, what had been his conduct to his nephew—could call him a warm friend, but on the other hand he was a bitter enemy. Even in Park Lane, where he had been but a hanger-on of Edgar's, he had resented the being treated on terms of equality by the young Government clerk: it may be imagined therefore how, as the husband of Lady Orr, and the practical possessor of a princely income, he resented it now. I am afraid, indeed, if there was any change in the behaviour of Charley towards him, it was the other way, as though he thought him a greater sneak than ever. Of the two classes of individuals, one of which ' thinks all the world belongs to them,' and the other ' does not care twopence whom it belongs to,' the latter has clearly the advantage: they are equally independent, and have no ' position ' to keep up. Ralph's assumed dignity never sat so ill upon him as when he opposed it to the arrows of Charley's scorn.

His host's tolerance of the young fellow's impudence, as Ralph termed Charley's natural ways, disgusted him ; Mrs. Peyton's obvious tenderness for Charley, Mary's evident goodwill, which might any day blossom into love, irritated him exceedingly ; but what made him well-nigh beside himself with rage (and the more so because it was necessary to conceal it) was the affection which Lady Orr herself, more openly than all, showed to this young man. He had always been a favourite with her, till he had almost lost her good graces by his dislike of the Dornays, and his partisanship of Mary's cause against herself. The latter she had forgotten and forgiven—nay, had even confessed to herself that he had been in the right in the matter; while his views in the former case, being now her own, were an actual claim upon her sympathy. To her husband's eyes, all proofs of her goodwill to Charley were a reflection upon himself.

'How right you were, my dear boy,' they seemed to say, 'in your estimate of the man I have been so mad as to marry!'

Under these circumstances, it will easily be understood in whom Dr. Bilde found an ally in his plans against the young Government clerk, and indirectly against Mary. It was, as I have said, to his surprise, for the Doctor of course was ignorant of Ralph's reasons for hating Charley; but, having found how the land lay, he lost no time in putting his schemes into effect. When scoundrels do agree, their unanimity (till its particular object is attained) is extraordinary.

Though her son was at the Hall, Mrs.

Sotheran herself was not a frequent visitor there ; not so much because the Happy Family were by no means to her taste, as from sheer terror of the possible consequences that might arise at any moment from a certain matter in which she had had an unwilling hand ; but Charley was naturally often up at Bank Cottage, and not the less so, we may be sure, that Mary was a frequent visitor there. It was a characteristic of the nervous little widow that she had never spoken to the girl, since her arrival at Letcombe Dottrell, on the matter of which she had written to her from Park Lane. She shrank from the subject, very literally, ' with fear and trembling,' and it was one which Mary also had no desire to broach. On the other hand, it was a ' comfort ' to Mrs. Sotheran—that morbid sort of satisfaction which persons of her temperament feel in details of personal misfortune—to talk about her own past life to the girl. The scene of these conversations was often the little churchyard, where, with their graves around her, she would discourse of her dead husband and her dead children; of the 'toiling and moiling' incident to supporting a large family upon a small income; of the difficulties she had had in making both ends meet; and of the anxiety she felt about Charley's future. He was the best son that mother ever had, and instanced some examples—how, for one thing, he had helped out of his scanty salary to pay her debts—which certainly tended to prove it.

'I never doubted Charley's goodness,' replied Mary, on one occasion, in answer to some similar eulogy.

'Nor I yours, my dear,' answered Mrs. Sotheran, with a deep sigh; and then, very inconsequently as it seemed, added, 'It is a hard world.'

If one had filled up the hiatus between these observations, it would have run thus: 'Being two such excellent young people, what a pity it is that cruel circumstances have put it out of your power to become one!' I do not say that Mary's blush proved that she had understood as much, but she believed that Mrs. Sotheran would have been glad to call her daughter, save for the obstacle of that stigma of her birth; whereas if she could have read that lady's thoughts, it was not its stigma but the peculiar circumstances of it, at which she dared not even hint. In comparison with this, the fact of the young folks having no means to marry upon was a small matter. As to Mary's own feelings with respect to Charley, they had certainly changed since the days when Mrs. Beckett had written to his mother, ' You need not be alarmed about Mary's falling in love with your boy.' She had at that time, as we know, another attachment; and though, even when that was broken off, she had not looked on Charley with eyes of love, she had of late begun to regard him very favourably. His independent character, his hatred of wrong and cruelty, and that courage of his opinions which he never failed to display against any odds, and to the danger of his own interests, filled her with secret admiration. It is probable, too, that the perseverance of his devotion did not count for nothing : continual dropping wears away the very granite, and a maiden's heart is of the sandstone formation. Nevertheless, Mary took care to reply to Mrs. Sotheran's observation, 'It is a hard world,' though it was obviously made with a particular significance, in a general sense.

'Yes,' she sighed, ' the world *is* hard, especially to the poor. I often think that the good people who eulogise work so highly do not know much of over-work.'

'Quite true,' assented Mrs. Sotheran. ' Poor Sarah Dempster yonder (she pointed to a neighbouring tombstone) was of your opinion : her epitaph, unlike those of most of us, paints her life as it really was. If you never read it, it is worth your while to do so.'

The tombstone stood in a neglected corner of the churchyard, overgrown with nettles and long grasses, but its inscription was still legible.

Here lies a poor woman, who always was tired,
Who lived in a house where help was not hired ;
Her last words on earth were: 'Dear friends, I am going
Where washing ain't done, nor sweeping, nor sewing ;

But everything there is exact to my wishes,
For where they don't eat there 's no washing up dishes.
I 'll be where loud anthems will always be ringing,
But, having no voice, I 'll get clear of the singing.
Don't mourn for me now, don't mourn for me never,
I 'm going to do nothing for ever and ever.'

'That may not be poetry,' observed Mrs. Sotheran, with unconscious plagiarism, 'but it 's true. There is nothing much worse than over-work.'

'Except shame,' said Mary, bitterly.

The sentiment, coming as it seemed from the girl's very heart, could not be ignored.

'There is no shame where there is no sin,' put in the other in a trembling voice.

'How can there be no shame when one has a past that one dares not look upon?—when one has a secret of which one dares not speak?'

'Hush, hush, for Heaven's sake!' whispered her companion, vehemently.

Upon the late Mrs. Dempster's headstone, which Mary was still regarding, there was projected a tall shadow, and the harsh voice of Dr. Bilde was heard exclaiming, 'Good morning, Mrs. Sotheran: I hope I am not interrupting your meditations among the tombs.'

CHAPTER XXXIX.

AN EXCITEMENT IN THE HAPPY FAMILY.

THE effect of Dr. Bilde's sudden and unforeseen appearance was considerable upon both the ladies, though very different in degree. To Mary he was always objectionable, and the present circumstances were little adapted to set him off to advantage. His cynical face and sneering tones seemed singularly out of place in the quiet little churchyard, whither, to her knowledge, he had never come before. She would almost as soon have expected to see him in the church itself. It has been said of another gentleman with a scientific turn that he would 'peep and botanise upon his mother's grave,' but it is probable that Dr. Bilde would have gone to even greater lengths in the cause of science, without scruple. The idea of eavesdropping did not occur to Mary in connection with him, not because she did not think him base enough, but because no motive for it suggested itself to her mind; but the recollection of her own last words (not to mention that 'Hush, hush, for Heaven's sake!' of her companion) did make her not a little uneasy.

If he had heard them, whether by accident or design, they could hardly have escaped his attention, and she was almost sure he had heard them. Mary's mortification and annoyance were very great; and, if she had been at liberty to follow her own instincts, she would have been content to acknowledge the doctor's presence by a bow, and then left him to 'meditate among the tombs' by himself. But the agonised and terrified expression of Mrs. Sotheran's face was an appeal she could not resist, and she resolved to take the doctor off the poor lady's hands at whatever cost to herself. The consciousness that she could do so very easily made the task, however, no less disagreeable to her, but the reverse. She knew instinctively—though he had been always hostile in his manner to her rather than otherwise—that she had some sort of attraction for him; and she did not hesitate, for her companion's sake, to make use of it for the first time.

'We are looking at Sarah Dempster's epitaph,' Mary observed, as if in reply to the doctor's observation. 'Your habits of hard work will scarcely permit you to sympathise with it, I fear.'

He came up to her at once and read the lines aloud in his metallic voice.

'That last line, "I am going to do nothing for ever and ever," is a bold one,' he remarked, 'and might well incur Mr. Wells's orthodox probation.'

'But consider how the poor woman must have toiled and slaved in this life,' observed Mary.

'True; but where the sting lay was that she toiled alone; the headstone says, "Sarah Dempster, Spinster." She was forty-five, which is my own age exactly; and all these years she had probably no one to sympathise with or assist her, which is my own case.'

'I should have thought you were the last person to need sympathy, or, if I may say so without offence, even to understand it,' said Mary, frankly.

'You may say anything to me without offence,' returned the doctor, in his usual measured tones. 'I am sometimes disappointed with what I hear you say, but never offended. As to sympathy, in the common acceptation of the term, I confess I do not value it: it seems to me a method by which one nature strives to weaken another, at its own expense, by union; whereas the very intention of union is, or should be, an accession of strength.'

'Please remember, Dr. Bilde, that, as you told Mr. Hindon the other day, I am not intellectually a swimmer, and therefore should not be taken out of my depth.'

'You would swim very well, Miss Marvon, if you would only accept a little teaching,' said the doctor, gravely. 'There is no woman I have ever met of whose intelligence I have formed so high an opinion.'

Mary made him a sweeping curtsey, with the object not so much of acknowledging his politeness as of having an excuse for turning half round and discovering whether Mrs. Sotheran had made her escape. To her great relief, she found that she had done so.

'If you imagine I paid you a compliment, Miss Marvon, you are mistaken,' continued the Man of Science. 'I would not do your noble nature such a wrong.'

'I am afraid, Dr. Bilde, that you overrate my nature, or, rather, mistake it altogether for something that it is not.'

'Pardon me, it is you yourself who mistake it. It has capabilities of which you do not guess, if you would but give them a fair chance —if only you would accept of instruction.'

'Thank you, Dr. Bilde,' said Mary, moving away towards Bank Cottage as to the nearest harbour of refuge, 'but my education is finished.'

'Nay, Miss Marvon, it is not even begun. A day may come perhaps, and at no distant date, when it may be more worth your while to listen to me——'

' Worth my while, Dr. Bilde ? '   There had been such an unmistakable menace in his tone that it was impossible to ignore it ; and Mary Marvon was not a girl to be menaced.   As she stood before him, with raised head and flashing eye, she disproved the poet's dictum, that the swan is born to be ' the only graceful shape of scorn.'

' I did not use the expression in a worldly sense,' explained the doctor, earnestly.   He would have even touched her shoulder with his hand, approvingly, had she not withdrawn herself out of reach. ' You must not identify me with those sordid, grasping souls among whom we move down yonder. The time comes to every one of us, though sometimes too late, when it seems worth our while to be wise.'

He lifted his hat in farewell as he spoke, for Mary was moving quickly away towards

Bank Cottage. His words had altogether failed to mitigate her indignation, or to do away with the impression that he had meant to threaten her. Nay, the very fact of his having endeavoured to excuse himself, strengthened her conviction, because excuse and apology were so foreign to his tongue.

Of this, however, she said nothing to poor Mrs. Sotheran, whom she found disturbed enough at this meeting with Dr. Bilde already; only, instead of being indignant as Mary was, she seemed almost out of her mind with terror.

'What on earth could the man mean by stealing after us in the churchyard like a cat?' said Mary.

'Don't say a cat, my dear,' shuddered the widow: 'the cat comes after mice. "How can there be no shame," you said, "when one has a secret of which one dares not speak?" Heaven grant he did not hear you!'

'And what if he did hear me?' asked Mary, boldly.

'Oh, my dear, don't speak of it!' cried

Mrs. Sotheran, wringing her hands with a passionate distress that, to the girl, seemed exaggerated, if not inexplicable. ' Let us hope for the best, and try to forget it. Thank Heaven, here 's Charley coming up the lane.'

Charley indeed could not mend matters—could not even with prudence be informed that matters wanted mending—but it was a comfort to them both to see him. His pleasant face, however, did not look quite so bright as usual.

' I bring great news with me,' he said, addressing his mother, but with a significant glance at Mary, as though the news affected her rather than Mrs. Sotheran. ' Mr. Rennie has arrived.'

' I am so glad,' cried Mary, clapping her hands.

' I dare say you are,' said Charley, viciously, ' but you needn't show that you are glad : I call it positively indelicate.'

' What do you mean ?' inquired Mary. ' Why should I not be glad that Mr. Rennie has come? He has been a very good friend to me, and I like him immensely.'

'This is what I call "owdacious!"' exclaimed Charley, holding up his hands: 'a most striking instance of that description of gratitude which is defined as the sense of favours to come. Is it possible you don't know what he's come about?'

'How on earth should I know?'

'Here's an unconscious Miss Kilmansegg! —*You* understand, at all events, mother, why Mr. Rennie has come down to Letcombe? He has been here often enough on the same errand.'

'Oh dear, oh dear!' gasped Mrs. Sotheran; 'I suppose it's a new will.'

'Well, of course it is, and Mary here is to have a million.'

'How can you talk such nonsense, Charley!' cried Mary, laughing.

'Well, of course I may be wrong as to the exact sum, but I only repeat what everybody else is saying. The flutter among the Happy

Family down yonder is something beyond precedent. Even Dr. Bilde, whom I have just met, and who is sure of his codicil, seemed immensely interested, and turned back to the Hall instead of going for his usual constitutional, in hopes, I suppose, to pick up some crumbs. I asked Mr. Nayler whether he thought Mr. Rennie was a presentment, or a flesh-and-blood solicitor, and you have no idea how angry he was.'

'How can you be so foolish, Charley, as to make enemies of all these people?' observed Mary, reprovingly. 'They may do you a bad turn some day.'

'Enemies!' replied Charley, comically; 'why, they are very dear friends of mine; or at least they were until just now. This news, I suppose, has put them a little off their heads. I did but ask Mr. Marks, *à propos* of Mr. Rennie's arrival, whether personal property, and how to dispose of it, was to be found in the Categories, and he immediately lost his temper. I never heard him express himself so concisely before.'

'I am afraid you must have said something to anger Mr. Marks very much,' said Mary; 'you seemed such a favourite of his. It is a great pity to quarrel with any one.'

'There couldn't have been a quarrel,' pleaded Charley, 'because it takes two to make one; and I was as cool as a cucumber throughout. At first, more like a physician than a metaphysician, he gave me some most excellent advice, and, at parting, what vulgar people call a piece of his mind, which, when one considers that he has none too much of it himself, was, as I told him, a very generous act.'

Mary looked very serious; nor was her distress alleviated by Mrs. Sotheran's whispered assurance that if dear Charley had quarrelled with Mr. Marks she might depend upon it that it was on her (Mary's) account.

'I shall go down to the Hall at once,' said Mary. 'I am sure there is mischief going on there, which may mean trouble to dear Mrs. Peyton.'

'Heaven forbid!' cried Mrs. Sotheran, fervently.

'If Miss Kilmansegg will graciously condescend to accept of my escort,' said Charley, 'I'll go with her. May I, Mary?'

'If you promise not to talk nonsense, you may, sir.'

As soon as they were alone together the young man became serious enough. He was not to be shaken, however, in his conviction that Mr. Rennie had been sent for upon Mary's account, and described the excitement at the Hall as something portentous.

'I most sincerely hope and trust, Charley, that you are quite mistaken,' said Mary.

'So do I,' returned Charley. 'I should be unworthy the name of man—which is a synonym for selfishness—if I didn't.'

'Why so?'

'Because if you are to have a million, or even half a million, you will be " in a cloud of gold, on a throne," no more to be approached by humble mortals such as myself.'

'How can you be so silly? I don't believe one word of such rubbish. But why should Mr. Peyton think of leaving me anything at all?'

'Nay, I can't blame him for that: in his place I should do the same, only much more so. I should order a waggon and fill it with title-deeds, and scrips, and shares for you at once; only, just as you were driving away with them, I should say, " Hi! you have forgotten something; it is not of much consequence, but won't you take me into the bargain?"'

'I thought you promised me not to talk nonsense, sir.'

'Quite true: I acknowledge it would be a very foolish proposition,' said Charley, humbly, and heaving a little sigh. 'Here is the grand almoner coming up the hill to meet you.'

It was certainly the fact that the lawyer was approaching them from the Hall; and from the manner in which he raised his hat to Mary, she felt an uneasy presentiment that she was the object of his mission.

CHAPTER XL.

MR. RENNIE'S LITTLE MISTAKE.

THERE was a sadness in Charley's 'Good-bye, Mary,' as he quitted her side and plunged into the shrubbery, before Mr. Rennie could bring his glasses to bear upon him, that seemed to give that gentleman's approach an additional significance; while the expression of the lawyer's face as he drew near betokened that he was the bearer of some important tidings. For the first time Mary began to think that there was really something of truth in Charley's wild words, and the idea was very far from giving her pleasure. Secure of the affections of Mrs. Peyton, and living for the most part in her society, life at the Hall had been on the whole agreeable to her; none of the members of the Happy Family were, however, to her taste, and what made them most objectionable to her was the greed and expectation with which they almost without exception regarded their host-patron. She was utterly unconscious of having already excited their jealousy or apprehension, but she foresaw that if it indeed were true that Mr. Peyton entertained any beneficial design in her favour, she would very speedily incur them. She felt she had no claim upon his bounty, nor (notwithstanding her experience of the ills of poverty) did she seem to herself to deserve it ; far from being one of those natures with whom material advantage compensates for everything, even to the loss of self-respect, she would have been unwilling to accept it, burthened with the envy of a single fellow-creature.

The lawyer's greeting was very cordial. In answer to her inquiries, he informed her that his health was tolerable, but that in business affairs he was unprosperous on account of the

loss of his chief copying clerk. His countenance was so admirably preserved, that for
the moment she was deceived, and only expressed a puzzled condolence. Then the
corners of his mouth began to twinkle, and
she perceived that he was referring to her own
professional services.

'Oh,' she said, 'you mean the type-writer.'

'To be sure I do. Do you suppose we
do not miss you at the office?'

'I can do some work for you now if you
are very hard pressed,' she answered, smiling;
'the machine is here.'

'If Mr. Peyton knew of it, I fear he would
set you to work with it. He makes a will a
week or so, in ever so many folios.'

'I don't want to have anything to do with
his will,' said Mary.

'That is monstrous, Miss Mary, and, in an
inhabitant of Letcombe Hall, even unnatural.
What do people come here for except to be in
Mr. Peyton's will?'

'You are rather sweeping in your judgments, Mr. Rennie,' said Mary, with ever so little of a flush. 'Do you suppose that Lady Orr, for example, wants Mr. Peyton's money?'

'To be sure, I had forgotten Lady Orr. She wishes, no doubt, that she had had less money rather than more, poor woman. And there's her St. Bernard, Alexander. I admit that neither of them wishes to be a legatee.'

'Well, surely Mr. Ralph Dornay has no ambition of that sort?'

'Indeed I don't say that; he has no expectation, but I should say he had a very considerable ambition. It is difficult to choke a dog with pudding.'

'I am afraid his wife is very unhappy,' said Mary, gently.

'Of course she is, being what the gentlemen of my profession who are connected with the criminal branch of it term "a Lifer." Great as is her punishment, however, it is hardly greater than the folly she committed. Marriages may be made in heaven originally, but I am inclined to think, after the first two or three, that they are turned out in another place. This third one of Lady Orr's certainly was. By-the-by, Miss Mary, that is the very subject I am come out to talk to you about—though not, I am sorry to say, at first hand. It is a commission. Do you happen to be thinking of marrying anybody, my dear young lady?'

'What a question!' exclaimed Mary, with a blush and a laugh.

'Just so. If I were not such an old friend, you are thinking to yourself, it would be almost a rude one.'

'I think, Mr. Rennie, that you are incapable of a rudeness,' put in Mary.

'I am more obliged to you for that assurance than I can express,' pursued the lawyer, earnestly. 'I am most fortunate in finding you alone. Would you mind stepping into the shrubbery—there is a seat yonder, if I remember rightly—so that we can speak together without fear of interruption? You have good sense as well as good feeling, my dear young lady, and you will understand that in what I am about to say I am only obeying the instructions of a very uncommon sort of client. If his object were not to benefit you, I should certainly not be his intermediary in this matter; but he was averse to speak of it (as he might well be) with his own lips, and I flattered myself that, since it must needs be broached, it would be less distasteful from those of an old friend. I need scarcely tell you that I speak on behalf of Mr. Beryl Peyton. Since you have been here so long, you can hardly be surprised at any eccentricity on Mr. Peyton's part. His impulses, though more rapid than his prejudices, are not less vehement, while in carrying them into effect he knows not the meaning of the word "impossible." You must promise me, my dear Miss Mary, that as you will not be astonished, so you will not be angered by anything he has made it my task to say to you.'

'I will do my best, Mr. Rennie, to behave

as you would wish,' said Mary, gently ; ' but I confess you a little alarm me.'

'There is no necessity for alarm. All that you need is to know your own mind,' said the lawyer, impressively. 'It will not be moved, if I have read it aright, by any considerations of advantage, to do your woman's heart a wrong. I am not expressing myself as I would wish, Miss Mary. If I were drawing up your marriage settlement I should feel more at home.'

'There is nothing amiss in your choice of words,' said Mary, in a low tone. 'Since you must needs do so, pray go on.'

'It is something that the Court, so far, is with me. Mr. Peyton has taken it into his head that with a slight effacement of time, if not of space, he can make two lovers happy. You are one of them.'

'I !'

'Certainly. You first and the other afterwards. The feminine in this case is much more worthy than the masculine. The fact is, Mr. Peyton has taken an immense liking to you, my dear Miss Mary, for which I do not blame him in the least ; but, as always happens when he has conceived an affection for any one, he wishes to take matters out of the hands of Providence, and to arrange them himself.'

'That is to say, I suppose,' said Mary, quietly, 'that I am to be made happy after his own fashion, or that I am not to be happy at all.'

'No,' replied Mr. Rennie, quickly, 'to do Mr. Peyton justice, this is not a question of accepting his benevolence or losing his favour. I wish you particularly to understand that. You are altogether a free agent. I have, it is true, a guerdon in one hand, but I have no menace in the other. That is a position in which I am unhappily often placed, but no consideration on earth would induce me to approach you with a menace. I asked you just now whether you were thinking of marrying anybody—a question, I perceive, not to be answered. Still, the interests affected by your reply are so enormous, that I am bound to be importunate. Let me put it, with all respect and delicacy and in the strictest confidence, another way. Is there any one under Mr. Peyton's roof who, you have reason to believe, is attached to you, and whose affection, if declared, you think it possible you might reciprocate?'

The question would have been an embarrassing and even a distressing one to any young woman, but to Mary it was peculiarly so. She confessed to herself that there was such a person at Letcombe Hall, but as she had until lately experienced no such feeling towards him, and had even forbidden him to speak of love to her, how could she entertain the possibility of becoming his wife, or even speculate on such a matter to a third person? She therefore remained silent.

'Let me make it easier for you,' said Mr. Rennie, gently. 'Is there any young gentleman under yonder roof who at one time flattered himself with the hope of securing you, and whom only the consciousness, or the impression, that there is no hope, prevents from continuing his attentions?'

To this most young ladies in Mary's position would have replied, if they had made reply at all, 'There may be.' It was characteristic of that young lady that she answered more directly, though in hesitating and unwilling accents, 'Yes, there is.'

'So I have been given to understand,' said the lawyer, gravely. 'Now, supposing that this young gentleman should be encouraged to renew his suit, is there any reasonable hope that he would meet with better success with you? Do not distress yourself by answering me, Miss Mary,' put in the lawyer, after a little pause; 'your truthful face gives your reply. Since I have obtained it, there is now no harm in telling you the great things that are in store for you. It was my duty, perhaps, to have spoken of them earlier, but I well knew they would not affect your choice; and it is right to add that, since the young gentleman in question is no

better informed upon the matter than yourself,
they can in no way have affected his.'

Into Mary's blushing face there stole a little
smile which seemed to say, ' That is an assurance which I did not require.'

' It is Mr. Peyton's intention to make your
husband an allowance of two thousand pounds
a year, and to secure to you absolutely by will
a sum of money, of which it is, perhaps, only
necessary to say that it is of very considerable
amount. My word for that,' he added, in reply
to a puzzled look on Mary's face, ' is sufficient,
is it not? Or do you want the details ? '

' My dear Mr. Rennie,' exclaimed Mary,
without paying attention to this last remark,
which indeed she did not even hear, ' your proposition is so amazing to me from first to last
that I can hardly believe I am not dreaming.
If I could see the slightest reason for this extraordinary munificence, I should be better able
to acknowledge it.'

' Reason ? That is the very last thing you
will get from Beryl Peyton. But I may tell

you, for your comfort, that I have known him
do much stranger things.'

'Is Mrs Peyton aware of these intentions?'
inquired Mary, earnestly.

'It is very unlikely. Her husband is not
communicative to her on matters of business.'

'Then, without her approval, Mr. Rennie,
beyond expressing my deep sense of Mr.
Peyton's unexampled generosity, which ex-
ceeds alike my desires and my merits, I can
make you no reply to his princely offer.'

It was characteristic of the girl, and impressed the lawyer very much, that the brilliant
prospect thus suddenly unfolded to her gaze,
while it naturally astonished, had failed to
dazzle her. It was not the first time by many
that it had fallen to his lot to inform persons of
some great and unexpected prosperity, and the
effect had been always rapture unalloyed by
scruple. The notion now conveyed to him by
Mary's behaviour was that the object of her
choice was not a favourite with Mrs. Peyton,
and he seized upon the opportunity (which

indeed he had long desired) to speak a word of warning.

'My dear young lady, it is to the last degree unlikely, from what I know of your hostess, that she will stir a finger to oppose your happiness. On the contrary, even if she has objections, she will rather stretch a point and waive them in order to secure it. This is a matter that can only be settled by your own inclinations. If you are sure of them, well and good; if you are not sure—still more if you have secret doubts of the man to whom you are about to intrust your future—you will— I hardly know how to speak of such a thing without offence, and I know it sounds like an address to a jury—but you will give yourself the benefit of them.'

'As to that, I am quite sure I have no doubts,' said Mary, smiling faintly.

'Very good,' replied the lawyer, though the expression of his face was even graver than before. 'It is not in my instructions, and indeed would be directly contrary to the spirit of them, to suggest impediments. You will have a bridegroom as handsome as his fortune; and there is this to be said, that the connection will draw you still nearer to an old friend of yours, whose friendship is worth having—Lady Orr.'

' Yes,' said Mary, smiling as a woman smiles when she is speaking of those who appreciate the man she loves, ' it is a great pleasure to me that Lady Orr is so fond of Charley.'

' Fond of who?' said the lawyer, forgetting his grammar in his astonishment. ' Did you say Charley?'

'I have always called him Charley,' admitted Mary, softly. ' If—if matters should turn out as you have proposed, there will be nothing to wish altered, I am sure, as regards Lady Orr.'

' Oh, well, I don't know much about such things,' said the lawyer: ' I suppose, as any stick will do to beat a dog with, any term of affection comes handy to indicate the beloved object; but, as a matter of fact, and as I've got it down in my instructions, the young gentleman's name is Edgar.'

'Edgar!' exclaimed Mary, turning scarlet. 'Do you mean Mr. Edgar Dornay?'

'Why, who on earth else should it be? Good gracious! what have I done?' for the blood had left the young girl's cheeks as quickly as it had rushed into them. 'My dear Miss Mary, I am sure that a sensible young woman like you is never going to faint. For my sake—for Heaven's sake— don't faint!'

Even the lawyer's agonised appeal might have failed to restore Mary to herself, had not her pride come to her aid.

'There has been some terrible mistake,' she murmured.

'But who else *is* there?' exclaimed Mr. Rennie. His eyes were open wider than they had ever been before, and yet he could not see where his error lay. 'It isn't one of the Happy Family, surely. *Not* Mr. Marks, *not* Mr.

Nayler; it can't be Mr.—what's-his-name—
that lies so?'

'No, Mr Rennie, indeed it is none of those
gentlemen,' gasped Mary, between a sob and a
laugh.   'It 's Charley Sotheran.'

'But I said the man was *here*, staying at
the Hall.'

'Well, Charley has been staying here these
three weeks.'

'Then why didn't that ridiculous old
lunatic—that is to say, I mean my excellent
client—vouchsafe to say so?' exclaimed the
lawyer, with irritation.   'How should *I* know?
I was never placed in such a false position
in the whole course of my life.'

Mary answered nothing, but perhaps her
face said, 'And the position you have placed
me in is not a very pleasant one for a young
lady to find herself,' for her companion continued, in a less vehement tone, 'It is one of
the disadvantages flowing from an imperial
policy that even when these high-handed
gentry intend to do good, they as often as

not do harm from not taking into account the feelings and desires of other people. I owe you an apology, my dear young lady, for having precipitated matters—for that is the worst that can happen—with Charley.'

'Good Heavens! you will not do anything so outrageous as to tell him, Mr. Rennie?' exclaimed Mary, in consternation.

'Of course not, of course not,' replied the lawyer, with a promptness in itself not a little suspicious; and, in point of fact, the notion of telling Charley had at once occurred to him as the most obvious means of reparation for his mistake. 'The secret shall be your own—as long as you can keep it. Yes, yes, and I shall take care that Charley's interests, since they are also yours, shall take no hurt from this little misapprehension. I have been made a fool of, but I will not be made a tool of; and though you may not be made an heiress, you shall get something out of the fire.'

'Indeed, Mr. Rennie,' put in Mary, earnestly, 'I beg you will not dream of making any application to Mr. Peyton on my account.'

'Very good: that is as you please, young lady; what I shall say to him then will be upon *my* account. Business is business; to have been sent upon a fool's errand like this is not what I bargained for. However, I have one consolation, Miss Mary, which buoys me up; I 'll add it to the bill.'

In spite of Mary's distress of mind, which was considerable, she could not repress a smile at the old lawyer's indignation, and at his self-suggested means of mitigating it. In his case, whatever conflagration arose in the way of trouble and misapprehension, it was clear the fire-engines were always on the spot. The very idea of a fine bill of costs seemed at once to soothe him, and turn his thoughts into a kindly channel.

'There is one thing, Miss Mary, in this unfortunate affair,' he continued, ' which, if you will allow me to say so, gives me genuine satisfaction. I am very glad that it *is* Charley.

It is true I don't know much about him, but I
am a believer in the doctrine of averages, and
the odds are that he's a better fellow than
Edgar.   He mayn't be much to look at—I beg
pardon, I mean so handsome as the other—
wrong again, am I?'—and indeed the expression of his companion's face most unmistakably
showed that there were two opinions on that
point. 'What a precious mess I'm making of
it!' exclaimed poor Mr. Rennie, wiping his
forehead with his pocket-handkerchief. 'If I
don't put it at three figures, may I be struck off
the Rolls! What I wish to say, Miss Mary,
without prejudice (there, now I'm at home
again), is, that Handsome is as Handsome does,
and you will do me the justice to say that while
dwelling on the personal advantages of Mr.
Edgar Dornay, I never uttered one word of
recommendation of him.   As he is my client
no longer, I am free to confess that I think you
have done very wisely.   I don't know why it
is, that a devotion to Music, Poetry, and the
Fine Arts should always make a man so infer-

nally selfish, but so it is; and Mr. Edgar Dornay is, in my opinion, no exception in his worship of No. 1.'

Here Mary looked so grave and pained that the lawyer came to a full stop. Had he known more of Charley he would willingly have praised him; but as it was, his means of conciliation—or what he thought would have the effect of conciliating—were confined to the depreciation of Edgar.

'I have nothing more to say, Miss Mary,' he added, ' save to express my regret—and my felicitations. If I could do anything to atone for my involuntary error——'

'You can be silent, Mr. Rennie,' put in Mary, significantly. 'Then the only person who will have suffered from your indiscretion will be myself.'

With that, she made him rather a ceremonious curtsey, and resumed her way to the Hall. Upon the whole, if it could not be said that she did well to be angry, it was certainly no wonder that she was annoyed at what had happened. No young lady likes the expression of her love to be wrung from her by a third person, and especially by mistake : it is one of the things she looks forward to, to tell that precious secret to the beloved object with her own lips, and Mr. Rennie had possessed himself of it—though, it is true, involuntarily—under false pretences. On the other hand, the lawyer by no means considered Mary to be the sole person aggrieved. 'The only person who will have suffered!' he echoed indignantly, as he watched her moving slowly, not to say haughtily, through the trees. 'Upon my life she's a cool hand. It is my experience that girls always *are* cool, except on those very matters when it most behoves them to keep their heads. The only person! As if the false position in which I have been placed—a respectable solicitor acting upon the most absurd instructions—was to count for nothing! How was I to know that it was Charley and not Edgar, unless indeed I ought to have taken it for granted that that wonderful client of mine was making some confounded mistake? Then who could doubt that it was Edgar, even from what the girl said herself? "Is there any one under Mr. Peyton's roof," I asked, "who, you have reason to believe, is attached to you?" And again, "Is there not a young gentleman who once flattered himself with the hope of winning you?" And to each of those questions she answered "Yes." So it seems that both these young men have asked her to marry them, and are prepared to ask her again. Do they always do it twice, I wonder? If so,' added the lawyer, grimly, ' I can only say that I have done my best to restore the average by never having done it at all.'

CHAPTER XLI.

'ENGAGED.'

AT the court of a certain French king the position of a person at table was an index of his rising fortunes, and the nearer he was placed to the Royal Transparency, the nearer he seemed to be to heaven.   It was the same in some sort at Letcombe Hall, and certain changes at the dinner table, on the day of Mary's interview with Mr. Rennie, filled the minds of the guests with speculation.   By virtue of his office, Mr. Peyton's physician always filled the chair at his left hand, while the right, unless any special reason—always set down to favouritism—arose for other arrangements, was usually occupied by the last comer.   For many days Mr. Ralph Dornay had sat there without much arousing the common envy ; he had failed to improve his opportunities as his host's next neighbour, and, indeed, it was pretty well understood that Mr. Peyton only tolerated him out of regard to Lady Orr. Under other circumstances Mr. Rennie would now have succeeded him, when, lo and behold ! when the company took their places, Mr. Edgar Dornay held that coveted place. It was almost as significant as though Mr. Peyton had laid his hand upon the young man's head, and announced in public ' this is my heir' ; but then he had made so many heirs, not one of whom had succeeded to a sixpence. Moreover, the attention of the guests—in other words, their envy, hatred, and malice—were attracted in another direction ; for Mr. Charles Sotheran now occupied Edgar's place by Mary's side. This also, it was felt, was symbolical of much, and aroused an equal apprehension. Considering the learning and philosophy in which so many of the party were wrapt, it was amazing how prompt they were to comprehend the circumstances : and, indeed, the only

person who did not understand them was
Mr. Charles Sotheran himself—a fact, however,
which did not at all interfere with his thorough
enjoyment of them.

'Now I call this nice,' he murmured, as he
dropped into the arm-chair—they were all arm-
chairs in the Letcombe dining-room—indicated
to him by the major-domo ; and, as Mary did
not contradict him, it is probable that the new
arrangement did not displease her. To have
sat next to Edgar, after Mr. Rennie's revelation
to her, would at all events have been most
embarrassing. and, even as matters stood, they
were rather trying. Not a word had escaped
her lips to any one as to what had happened
that morning, but she had no means of guess-
ing how much others knew ; and that something was known or guessed was obvious to
her. Mrs. Peyton's manner to her was even
more affectionate than usual, Lady Orr's more
cordial, and that of her host more significant
than all. Once he caught her eye, and raised
his champagne glass. while his fine face seemed

to glow, not only with goodwill, but with a certain tender forgiveness. 'I have been mistaken,' it seemed to say, 'and I am sorry; but though you have declined my road to happiness, I hope you will reach it by some other way;' indeed, he even glanced at her next neighbour, as much as to say '*that* way.'

'I hope there is a great deal to eat,' said Charley, as he inspected the *menu*.

'I call that very greedy, sir.'

'You are right, as you always are,' he answered. 'I should like to sit here for ever and ever.'

Mrs. Welbeck, who sat on the other side of him, though partial to her food, thought this sentiment a little exaggerated, and appealed to Miss Price about it.

'Mr. Sotheran says that he should like to eat for ever and ever.'

'How like a man!' replied that social philosopher; 'their aspirations are always of the earth earthy. For my part, I hold dinner, like war, to be a necessary evil.'

'Oh dear, I think that is going much too far in the other direction,' said Mrs. Welbeck, regarding the slice of salmon that had just been placed before her with all the rapture of anticipation. 'We are told in the Bible to take a little wine for our—I mean medicinally—and to enjoy—though for my part I can never digest a pear—the kindly fruits of the earth.'

'Such matters do not concern me,' said Miss Price, contemptuously. 'I am thankful to say my motto is *Ad astra*.'

'If it were mine, I wouldn't mention it,' muttered Mrs. Welbeck, who was not classical. 'The idea of a woman at her time of life having " led astray " for her motto! What are you laughing at, Mr. Sotheran? Nothing! I wish I could laugh at nothing; laugh, they say, and grow fat, because it is healthy. Yet Mr. Ralph Dornay yonder is very fat, and never laughs at all.'

At this particular moment Mr. Ralph Dornay was certainly not laughing. He was furious at having been deposed by his nephew, and still more furious at seeing Charley placed next to Mary. Once or twice he looked across, doubtless for sympathy, to Dr. Bilde, and found none. That gentleman was going through his dinner with that methodical enjoyment peculiar to members of his profession, who, while warning others of the dangers of the table, seem to pluck from them the flower Safety. (Is it, I wonder, that their skill holds them harmless, or that, since hawks do not peck out hawks' een, they know they can be cured for nothing?) On the present occasion, indeed, the doctor seemed even better satisfied with himself and the ways of 'Order' than usual. Perhaps knowing that his codicil was secure, the legatorial anxieties which were obviously consuming those about him were not without their charms for him: the pleasures of advantageous comparison are, with certain natures, always enjoyable.

Messrs. Marks and Nayler had no such consolation. These philosophers had long ceased to flatter themselves that the broad domains and rich investments of Mr. Beryl Peyton would fall to them *en bloc*. On the first revelation of their systems to their host and patron, they may, indeed, have entertained ambitious dreams, but of late years they had confined their expectations to mere 'pickings'—the thousands, or perhaps tens of thousands, that form the fringe of a great estate, and, when not swallowed up by that rapacious monster the residuary legatee, fall, like the precious dew from heaven, upon judicious outsiders. The elevation, therefore, of Edgar Dornay to a place so near the throne (which, besides, was not un-expected) was by no means so distasteful to them as the new distribution of Mr. Peyton's lesser favours. It was clear to them that he had given his sanction to Charley's addresses to Mary, and that henceforth there would be a coalition of interests between those two young people. 'What is enough for one is enough for two,' is a very pretty proverb, and exceedingly encouraging to folks about to marry; but, as a matter of fact, Mary's claims

upon Mr. Peyton would be certainly more considerable as a bride than in her former position.
It seemed to them, in short, that she was about
to be dowered at their (prospective) expense ;
and, what was the bitterest reflection of all,
their successful rival Charley would have a
share in the robbery !   Mary had been quite
correct in supposing that Charley had not only
lost the favour, but incurred the enmity, of
both these gentlemen ; but she did not know
that she herself had been the cause of
quarrel.   It had always been difficult for the
young man to restrain his indignation when
they had been wont to speak of her in his
presence in their philosophic manner ; but the
arrival of Mr. Rennie, which, as they justly
concluded, betokened the advancement of her
fortunes with Mr. Peyton, had stung them into
' saying things ' of that young lady which were
not only unphilosophic but unparliamentary.
Curiously enough, they had taken the same
view, though from very different standpoints,
with regard to the effect of her prosperity as

Charley himself—namely, that it would place her so high above his reach as at once to extinguish his pretensions to her ; and, judging his feelings from what their own would have been under similar circumstances, they counted upon his sympathy with their plain speaking. The result was so deplorable that it would be painful to describe, and impossible, if we retained Charley's words, to print it.

Under these circumstances it is not surprising that the dinner-table conversation languished, and that Mr. Hindon found his opportunities of agreeing with everybody uncommonly few. In the drawing-room things were but little better, though Charley, who took his seat by Mary as a matter of course, never noticed that there was a screw loose ; on the contrary, that tendency to yawn which sometimes besets a young gentleman over the tea and toast was entirely absent, and he thought it a most charming evening.

The climax of his satisfaction, however, was yet to come. When the ladies retired, Mrs.

Peyton whispered that she had a word to say to him in her boudoir, to which he repaired with very commendable promptness. His hostess received him with a most benevolent smile, which had, nevertheless, a touch of sadness in it. She could not help reflecting, perhaps, that, had not fate ordered it otherwise, she might have been about to confer happiness upon a son of her own. Nevertheless, Charley was dear to her. and the son of her dearest friend.

' My dear boy,' she said with a gentle gravity, ' it is my mission to tell you that Mary Marvon has somewhat disappointed my husband as regards a certain scheme he had proposed to himself for her future benefit. It was his hope that she would have formed a union with Edgar Dornay, who, as you know, is a great favourite of his, and who in other respects would have been a very eligible suitor ; but from certain information which has reached him to-day, and into which it is not necessary to enter, Mr. Peyton has come to the conclusion that such

a match would be distasteful to her; that there
is, in short, an obstacle to it. Can you enlighten me as to what it is?'

Charley was not given to blushing—'I am
modest, but not shy,' was the account he was
wont to give of himself, and as to the shyness
he was certainly correct; but on the present
occasion he blushed like a blush rose.

'I should imagine, from what I know of
her character, that if Miss Marvon declines to
marry Mr. Dornay, it is because she doesn't
like him,' he answered simply.

'But that is only a negative objection, sir.
My husband's apprehension is that Mary is in
love with somebody else.'

'That is a question, my dear Mrs. Peyton,'
he replied, 'which I cannot venture to answer;'
and this time Charley blushed like a peony.

'I rather thought you might have ventured,'
said Mrs. Peyton, drily; 'it has struck me once
or twice that you had rather a fancy for her
yourself.'

'There you have wronged me, madam,'

said the young man, with a gravity that became his pleasant face exceedingly. 'It is no fancy that I have for Mary Marvon, but a love that will last my life.'

'And is Mary herself aware of this?'

'Oh yes, it cannot but be so; but she has forbidden me to speak of it.'

'I see,' returned Mrs. Peyton, smiling. It struck her that there were other ways of hinting at devotion than by speech, and that this young man had not refrained from using them. 'Still, though you may imagine that you know your own mind upon this matter, you know very little of Mary; about her antecedents, for example——'

'My dear madam, such things may be interesting to Professor Price,' put in Charley, impatiently: 'but where Mary comes from I care nothing. All that is of consequence to me is that she is *here*, and I am always wondering at it, for she seems more fit for heaven.'

'But, Charley,' said Mrs. Peyton, in slow

and sorrowful tones, 'there is another thing which it is my duty to tell you. Neither my husband nor Mr. Rennie are aware of it, but it is only right that whoever seeks to be Mary's husband should know it—Mary is illegitimate.'

'If I was in the Registrar Office that might have some interest for me,' said Charley, drily, 'but, as it happens, I am in the Probate Office. The incident appears to me to belong to another generation, and does not affect me in the slightest degree.'

If Mr. Peyton could have heard Charley speak those words and seen the look of scorn which was their fit accompaniment, it would have shaken Edgar Dornay upon his throne; for no sentiment could have pleased the master of Letcombe Hall so well. His wife, indeed, was almost as much gratified, though from quite another cause.

'You are a true lover, Charley,' she exclaimed admiringly. Then she knocked at the door which communicated with her own bedroom, and from it there issued Mary herself.

The girl looked very pale and quiet, like one prepared for any fate; and though on catching sight of Charley the colour rushed to her cheeks, the next moment her eyes turned with earnest steadfastness to Mrs. Peyton.

'I have fulfilled my mission, my darling,' said that lady, tenderly; then, turning to Charley, she continued: 'It was imposed upon me, as you know, by Mr. Peyton and not by this young lady, who, having forbidden you to speak of love, could indeed hardly have ignored her own veto. From what I know of both your hearts, you may speak now.'

'Mary knows I love her,' said Charley, softly; 'she has always known it.'

For one fleeting instant the expression of trust and tenderness in Charley's face was reflected in Mary's own; then she turned again to Mrs. Peyton and whispered tremulously, 'Does he know all—all that his mother told you?'

Mrs. Peyton nodded assent. It seemed as if that nod had been some ingenious piece of mechanism which released two expectant bodies and caused them to rush into one another's arms.

'This precipitation, my dears,' observed the old lady, in tones of amused reproof, 'is, for all you know, the very height of imprudence. If, as I must needs conclude, you consider your-selves affianced to one another, does it not strike you that, as a married couple, you will have very little to live upon?'

'What I doat upon,' observed Charley, with roguish gravity, 'is a long engagement.'

'In the present case that is out of the question, sir. In whatever he has resolved upon. my husband is impatient of delay, and it is his wish that you young people should be married almost immediately.'

'Rather than disoblige Mr. Peyton,' said Charley, promptly, 'I will sacrifice myself at the altar to-morrow.'

'It will not be so soon as that, sir, but it will be very soon. A certain allowance will be made to you by my husband on your marriage, and be continued during pleasure. I am quite confident that it will never be forfeited by any misconduct of your own, my dears, but as you are not without your enemies, and it is possible that Mr. Peyton's ear may be abused, I have requested Mr. Rennie to settle (should occasion arise for it, or in case of my demise) a little money of my own upon you; not much indeed, for I have not much to give, but enough to keep the wolf from the door. No, no, don't thank me,' she added hurriedly; ' don't speak of it.—My drops, Mary.'

With those words, uttered with feeble haste, Mrs. Peyton had fallen back in her chair, with a face so ghastly and significant of mental agony that poor Charley, a moment before almost beside himself with joy and gratitude, was frozen with horror, believing that his benefactress was about to die. Mary, however, had found the remedy for which the patient had inquired, and applied it on the instant, and in a minute or two consciousness and speech returned.

'I did not need this warning for myself,' she murmured, 'but it will prove to you, my dears, how uncertain is my hold on life. Mr. Rennie must bestir himself at once to give effect to my wishes.'

Mary threw herself on her knees and besought her hostess not to disturb her mind with anxieties on her account.

'If we could but see you well, my dear Mrs. Peyton, there would be nothing wanting to complete the happiness you have conferred upon us.'

'Would that it *were* conferred, dear girl!' was her unexpected rejoinder. 'What little span of life remains to me I would gladly give could I thereby insure it. Though the sun seems to shine on you to-day, the sky is full of clouds that threaten all of us. To part from you will be pain indeed, yet I would that you were already in some little home with Charley. So long as you remain beneath this roof, every breath you draw is perilous, every step you take is over pitfalls. I would warn you of them, but I dare not—— Hush, hush! is there not some one in my room?'

Mary stepped in quickly and examined the apartment. She, too, had fancied that she had heard the rustle of a dress close to the half-open door. But her search convinced her that she had been mistaken. Mrs. Peyton's alarm seemed also to have subsided, for, having dismissed Charley with a maternal embrace, she declined Mary's offer to share her apartment for the night.

'To have you near me, my dear, is a temptation such as you cannot guess,' she said, in trembling tones, ' but there is danger in it to us both.'

'What danger?' inquired Mary, wonderingly.

'Nay, you must not ask me that,' sighed the old lady, with a strange, fond look, which was at the time inexplicable to the girl. 'There is danger in your asking why. There is danger everywhere, both to you and to me.'

CHAPTER XLII.

ROSE-COLOURED.

IT was characteristic of Mr. Beryl Peyton, and of his rôle of Deputy Providence, that he himself never uttered one word respecting his good intentions to the two young people whom he desired to benefit. They were given to understand by Mr. Rennie that any expression of gratitude on their part would be even resented. There were many who had cause (or thought they had) to be disappointed with Beryl Peyton as a patron, but no one could accuse him of a broken promise, for he never made one. There were hundreds who had reaped his favours, and were still reaping them, but they were all bestowed (as his wife expressed it) 'during pleasure.' Sometimes his own right hand was unconscious of what his left hand gave, sometimes Mr. Rennie was the depositary of the secret, and sometimes (when there seemed a necessity for it) the information was shared by one or two others. In the present case it would have been better for the objects of his generosity had it been made more public; or rather, if its moderate limits, which rumour greatly exaggerated, had been understood. To some of the members of the Happy Family it seemed as though their all was in danger of being taken from them at the eleventh hour by these youthful interlopers, who had borne none of the burden and heat of the day. To have tilled the field of expectation, and sown it with the seed of subservience, was no light labour, and to see the harvest reaped by hands that had done no stroke of work in that way was intolerable. Mr. Hindon alone could bring himself to congratulate Charley on his brilliant prospects, which (notwithstanding his own little attempt on Mary's heart) he did with much frankness and effusion. An ordinary marriage gift, he said, would not sufficiently express his sentiments, but if its distance from the Probate Office should not prove insuperable, and the young couple could arrange to live in the neighbourhood of Great Grimsby, he had a house of his own there, the title-deeds of which it would give him sincere pleasure to make over to them on their wedding-day.

Lady Orr's congratulations took a shape probably more sincere, and certainly more practical.

'My dear Mary,' she said, 'the good news I hear concerning you has been from the first, as you well know, the wish of my heart. I was Charley's advocate, remember, when you had not learnt to so thoroughly appreciate him as you do now.' It was amazing how she kept her countenance (and her colour), considering the recollections which must surely have occurred to her when thus alluding to events that had happened in Park Lane; but a lady who has married three times is not easily ' put out ' by any association of ideas. 'What I should like to do (and what I would have done had you taken my advice when it was offered) would be to make you a really handsome dowry. There, you needn't look like that! As I am not going to do it, you may surely permit me the cheap luxury of a generous intention. Circumstances have occurred '—here her brow grew dark—' which would make my now indulging myself in such a pleasure difficult.'

There had been a stormy scene between Lady Orr and her husband concerning this very matter, of which Mary could not guess. He had forbidden his wife to spend her own money according to her own fancy. Nor was even that, though it must have humiliated her, the worst of it. In his hatred of these innocent young people he had been so imprudent as to show the seamy side of his whole character to the woman who had hitherto, for her own sake, abstained from investigating it. She had been indeed conscious that there were seams, but its rents and rags and patches had been displayed and shaken menacingly in her face. The whole fabric of his nature had given way; not like a woman's dress, 'at the gathers,' but in a manner which proved the stuff was rotten.

'I *could* do it,' she went on, in a sort of passionate soliloquy ; ' and if it should ever be essential to your happiness, I would do it ; but it would be difficult.'

'My dear Lady Orr, it distresses me exceedingly,' began poor Mary—

'That 's my selfishness, my dear,' put in the other vehemently. 'I ought to have known that it would distress you. Let us say no more about it. It annoys me indeed that I can only give you trinkets, but, such as they are, you know my love goes with them.'

She drew from her bosom (it struck Mary with an icy horror that she had not dared to bring it openly in her hand) a jewel-case, and handed it to Mary. As she did so, the case flew open, and, in displaying its contents, stopped Mary's thanks in the bud. She beheld a parure of diamonds—a necklace with pendant, and two bracelets, glittering like the sea in the sun.

' My dear Lady Orr, it is impossible,' said

the girl, stepping back from the tempting spectacle as though it had been some physical danger ; ' these diamonds must have cost a fortune. It is like your generosity to offer them ; but consider how out of place they would look on me.'

' Whom should they become better? ' answered the other, impatiently. ' It is your pride which rejects them, Mary, and prevents me from showing how much I love you.'

' No, Lady Orr, it is not my pride,' answered the girl, smiling, ' but only my sense of proportion.'

I am afraid neither lady was quite truthful : for in the case of the elder one, beside her love, there was a secret desire to make reparation ; while the magnitude of the gift was in reality at the bottom of Mary's disinclination to accept it.

' It is a hard thing,' said Lady Orr, bitterly, ' that I cannot give you what I would, and that what I can give you will not accept from me.'

'Do not say that, I implore you,' pleaded Mary : 'if you must needs give me something costly, give me the bracelet you wear every night——'

'I dare not,' interrupted the other, quickly ; then, in answer to Mary's wondering look, she added, in a hoarse and terrible whisper, ' he will be sure to miss it, and ask where it is gone. No, you shall have the pearls Sir Robert gave me. They will suit you best, for they are associated with nothing but love and honour ; and, alas! they do not now suit *me.*'

For the first time throughout her acquaintance with her, Mary beheld Lady Orr in tears : they were so foreign to her character, or rather to the position she had so long occupied above the stabs of Fate, that the sight distressed her companion as much as a man's tears would have done.

' Do not weep for me, Mary,' continued the other, vehemently ; ' forget that I have ever shown this weakness, or, if you remember it, do so as a memento that love and truth are all that are worth a woman's living for;' then, pressing her lips to the forehead of the frightened girl, she hurried out of the room.

It was understood, though no particular time was fixed for the marriage of the young couple, that it would take place at an early date, and in the meanwhile Mr. Rennie was very busy with deeds and parchments in a certain room that had been for years set apart for him at the Hall, and which Charley (little dreaming that he should ever have any concern with it) had been wont to term the Letcombe Probate Office. Prudence, as one cannot but have observed, was not a leading feature in Charley's character. He was not ' as grave as a judge,' nor were his utterances judicious. When a humorous idea struck him, he expressed it, no matter what subject suggested itself to the play of his fancy. It is one of the penalties men pay for the possession of humour, that it carries them away with it like a runaway horse, and sometimes over the flower-beds, or across the cucumber frame. Nothing, as the dull

folks maintain, is sacred from them, by which
it is meant that they are not even restrained by
considerations of self-interest from having their
joke. The character of Beryl Peyton was one
which in many points appealed to the best
sympathies of the young Government clerk : he
had indeed a hearty regard and admiration for
him, and it need not be added a very keen sense
of his personal kindness; but he had said
things of even Beryl Peyton in a good-tempered
way which were less reverential than amusing ;
and, what was worse, he had taken little heed
as to who were his hearers. It was the nature
of the young fellow to talk openly to everybody, and, unless he knew a man for a sneak
and a talebearer, to take him for an honest man.
This was an attribute of Charley's which recom-
mended him to a few, but made him unpopular
with that large class of persons who, not daring
to be natural themselves, look upon naturalness
in others as a liberty and an impertinence. And
it alarmed the more cautious of his friends.
Mrs. Sotheran indeed fairly trembled at her

son's light talk and independent ways. As his mother she admired it, and was sometimes compelled to laugh at Charley's fun in spite of herself, but it was her private opinion that he had not the money for it.

'When you have ten thousand a year, my dear,' she would sagely observe, ' you may say what you like ; but as it is, you talk too freely.'

To Charley, whose salary only increased at the rate of ten pounds per annum, it is not to be wondered at that this prospect of emancipation seemed so exceedingly remote that it was hardly worth regarding; yet he was by no means one of those young gentlemen who ' despise their mother when she is old.' Perhaps he had even an uneasy sense that she was right in this matter, but, at all events, he had striven to moderate the freedom of his tongue to please her. He might just as well have attempted to alter the colour of his eyes.

It was not without some sense of triumph, therefore, as well as of blissful content, that he had brought her the news of his engagement to

Mary Marvon, and of Mr. Beryl Peyton's generous intentions towards them; and, indeed, in spite of their frank and independent ways, the young couple seemed to have done exceedingly well for themselves. His mother folded him in her arms, and expressed her joy in a flood of silent tears. So far nothing could be more natural or like herself; but he waited in vain for one word of congratulation. There was an expression of doubt and even alarm in her eyes, mingled with their love and thankfulness.

'Do you not believe me, mother?' he said. 'Does my news seem too good to you to be true?'

'Yes,' she answered, snatching eagerly at his suggestion, 'that is it. I have not been accustomed to good tidings.'

'For the rest of your life I hope things will be different, dear mother,' he said. 'Hitherto you have only known loss: to-day you have a daughter given to you.'

'Not yet,' she sighed, with a look like a

hare who hears, or thinks she hears, the cry of the hounds. 'There is many a slip 'twixt the cup and the lip.'

Charley smiled and kissed her. It was not very cheerful to be received in this Cassandra-like style; but he was accustomed to his mother's ways, and always very patient and tender with her. 'We must all die, my dear, if you mean that,' he said; 'but nothing short of death will now separate me and Mary.'

'I hope not; I trust not,' she murmured. 'But you tell me that Mr. Peyton has not yet spoken to Mary. Does not that seem strange?'

'To me it seems uncommonly strange,' said Charley, 'especially since under the circumstances he might even expect a kiss. Mr. Rennie leads me to imagine (though that's a secret) that Mr. Peyton means to allow Mary 500*l.* a year.'

'And Mr. Peyton has not spoken to his wife about all this.'

'Well, I don't know why you should have assumed that, but so it is. Of course such behaviour is peculiar. When I am Mary's husband I shall tell her everything I think will interest her; but then Mr. Peyton *is* peculiar. If he has chosen to make Mr. Rennie his intermediary, what is that to us?'

'But there will be investigations—inquiries?'

'Mrs. Peyton and I have had a talk together,' said Charley, gravely, 'and everything has been said that needs to be said. She has told me about Mary's parentage, and all that. If the—well, what you have in your mind—doesn't matter to *me*, how on earth should it matter to Mr. Peyton? Come, come; don't take such gloomy views, mother, on the brightest day that has ever dawned on me. We are to be married from the Hall, Mr. Rennie tells me, and Mr. Peyton himself is to give Mary away. Only think of that!'

It was probable that Mrs. Sotheran thought a good deal of it, for, long after Charley had been dismissed with another rain of tears and kisses, she sat rocking herself in her chair

alone, and murmuring, with frightened face,
'To be married from the Hall, and given away
with his own hands! It is terrible; it is
frightful! They are treading upon the edge
of a precipice.'

CHAPTER XLIII.

CONSPIRATORS.

It will be easily understood that the terrace
walk on which Charley and Mr. Marks had
been wont to discuss metaphysics together now
knew them no more. Tutor and pupil were no
longer on amicable terms, though, strange to
say, the views entertained by Mr. Marks of
Charley were much less philosophic than those
with which Charley regarded *him*. The milk
of human kindliness must, however, flow somewhere ; and that of Mr. Marks, being diverted
from his lapsed young friend, turned to his
whilom enemy Mr. Nayler, and made quite a
pool about him. The terrace walk, as being
well out of earshot of the Hall, while on the
other hand it commanded a good view of all

intruders, was their favourite haunt. Side by side they would walk for hours, apparently in the greatest amity. It seemed, as Charley said, as though the millennium had arrived, when the weaned child and the cockatrice were on visiting terms, and the Noumenon had laid down with the Presentment. The bond that drew them together was a common hatred, which for temporary purposes, and while it lasts, serves its purpose as thoroughly as the tenderest tie. Nor was it confined to a single object. They did not hate Charley, who had declined their friendship, one whit less than they hated Mary, who had declined their love. It must be confessed that the young man had given them some provocation by trifling with their philosophy; but this they would never have discovered had they been left to themselves. A friend, though scarcely a good-natured one, had been so good as to point out in each case that Charley had been amusing himself at their expense. Such an outrage, indeed, seemed almost incredible, but he had contrived to convince them of it. Resentment, of course, does not enter into the philosophic mind; so far as they were personally concerned they would have been well content to leave the offender to such punishment as Order inflicts upon those who transgress her laws; but they could not remain deaf to the voice of public duty.

'I have no more personal enmity to this young man than to yonder cow,' said Mr. Marks to Mr. Nayler, as they trod the smooth gravel side by side.

'It is not a cow,' returned Mr. Nayler, who piqued himself on his accuracy, and was not near-sighted as Mr. Marks was: 'it is Japhet Marcom in a stooping position, gathering beet-root as usual in the garden. But the sentiment is independent of the metaphor; I share it; I too can lay my hand upon my heart, and assert that I entertain no feelings towards Charles Sotheran other than those of disappointment.'

'Feelings very natural and very justifiable,' said Mr. Marks, warmly. 'I am told that the manner in which he ridiculed your psychological theories behind your back was most reprehensible.'

'Not more so, as I am informed,' returned Mr. Nayler, 'than the amusement he created in thoughtless persons by his imitation of your metaphysical speculations.'

'Which he was by nature wholly incapacitated from understanding,' observed Mr. Marks, severely.

'No doubt, no doubt,' observed Mr. Nayler, gravely. 'He even admitted that much, though he fell into the error of supposing that they were intrinsically unintelligible : one must allow that he is sufficiently plain-spoken.'

'He is the most impudent young man in the world, sir, and at the same time the falsest,' put in Mr. Marks, indignantly. 'To think that he should have hoodwinked our excellent host, and thereby secured that material success which alone has any attraction for him, is enough to make one doubt of the principles of Order.'

'Without committing myself so far as to acknowledge them,' observed Mr. Nayler, cautiously, 'and reserving my judgment upon the whole matter as regards the entity of the individual in question——'

'Entity? How can you talk of entities when he is going off with the money?' broke in Mr. Marks, impatiently.

'Let us say rather he is about to go off,' returned Mr. Nayler: 'in human affairs there is, properly speaking, no present.'

'There's a future, at all events,' observed Mr. Marks, drily, 'and that will be made very comfortable for him.'

'That is not so certain, if Mr. Peyton should discover the young man's unworthiness. Do you remember his likening our esteemed host, on account of his personal appearance, to Tarquinius Superbus?'

'Now you mention it, I do seem to remember something of the kind,' said Mr. Marks, with a keen glance at his companion.

'The operations of the memory are most

interesting and remarkable,' observed Mr. Nayler: 'creation and reproduction are so nearly allied, that they may be almost said to be identical. Let us try and remember some more things.'

It must be said in justice to these two gentlemen that plots and stratagems were by no means in their line: the course of conduct they were now about to enter upon had been suggested to them by an individual of far less intellectual capacity, but of a more practical turn of mind—namely, Mr. Ralph Dornay. He had a theory about evidence, or rather as to the production of it, which might have gained for him a high position at the Old Bailey: his notion was that the alleged utterances of an accused person C should be rehearsed between two witnesses, A and B; testimony thus received a firmer shape and tone, and if A should attribute what B had quoted from C's mouth to C himself, it was an error on the right side, and strengthened the case for the prosecution. He had excused himself from all personal participation in the present scheme upon the ground of delicacy of feeling: Mr. Sotheran and he were known to be on ill terms, and he could, therefore, take no immediate part in his exposure and confusion. He had known the young man (he explained) when he had been paying his attentions to Miss Marvon under other circumstances: she had been at that time employed in a subordinate capacity by Lady Orr, but was a favourite of hers, and had had certain expectations. When these vanished, in consequence of the young lady's own misconduct, Mr. Sotheran had promptly withdrawn his pretensions, and, now that fortune once more smiled upon her, he had again come forward as a suitor. This was, briefly, the true state of the case. With a good-nature that was under the circumstances to be regretted, if not actually reprehensible, Lady Orr had decided to let bygones be bygones, which placed Mr. Ralph Dornay himself in a position of much embarrassment. While unable himself to appear in the matter, he could not in the interests of justice withhold the above information from those (as he understood) who were taking steps to prevent the generosity of Mr. Beryl Peyton being abused. As to Miss Marvon, the fact that she still enjoyed (however mistakenly) the favour of Lady Orr must seal Mr. Ralph Dornay's lips; but Dr. Bilde was in a position to supply them with certain facts concerning that young person which would probably make their course an easy one.

Dr. Bilde also kept himself in the background. It was contrary to his principles, which were paramount, to mix himself up with any kind of domestic scandal: his profession was that of a healer, and out of that sacred calling he declined to step. It was unnecessary to say that he was uninfluenced by mercenary considerations, and indeed that matter of the codicil seemed to make him independent of them; but he could not consent to risk the loss of Mr. Beryl Peyton's confidence in his professional judgment, by allowing his name to be connected with what no doubt was a most just and necessary inquiry, but which might be misconstrued as an intrigue.

So Messrs. Marks and Nayler danced (metaphorically) upon the terraced walk together, while Dr. Bilde and Mr. Ralph Dornay deftly pulled the strings. The time was a slow one, as was fit and proper with marionnettes of a philosophic turn, and not a step was taken without design. But as time went on, the two gentlemen themselves grew very familiar with one another, and discoursed together with an openness that, had there been any possibility of their being overheard, might have been dangerous, and would have been described, even by their allies, as too full of zeal. It never crossed their minds that they were being made catspaws; nor indeed was there any reason why it should be so, since neither the doctor nor Mr. Dornay could hope for the chestnuts. Their notion was that, having opened Mr. Beryl Peyton's eyes to the real character of the persons he designed to benefit,

they would lay him under an eternal obligation. It is possible that they also calculated
upon receiving a fee in proportion to the
success of the operation ; and it was certain
that there would be a good deal of money
'going '—that is to say, that a large sum intended for a certain purpose would be set free
for diversion into other channels. But this
was by no means the main motive of our two
philosophers. Their desire was to see justice
done—a noble instinct, but one that is never
more powerful than when we have a personal
grudge against those who are about to be its
victims.

Notwithstanding that time pressed, and
that in the meanwhile these righteous souls
must needs have been vexed by the contemplation of the happiness of the young couple,
who, unconscious of their doom, and callous,
as it seemed, to all remorse, were enjoying
themselves exceedingly, it was not till long
after the indictment was prepared that the
mode of presenting it in the proper quarter

could be decided upon. Mr. Marks, whose abstruse pursuits and speculations perhaps inclined him to shrink from publicity, was in favour of an anonymous letter, a mode of proceeding which has this peculiar advantage, that if it misses fire you can disown it, and even lay its composition on somebody else. But Dr. Bilde, who knew the excessive distaste of his patron for all underhand proceedings, so vehemently opposed this scheme that it was abandoned in the bud. Mr. Nayler was for a round-robin, which, being signed by each member of the Happy Family, would compromise everybody alike. But, as here again Dr. Bilde pointed out, beside the actual difficulty of getting the signatures, the affair would thereby be only advanced a single stage—it would all be allegation and no proof, until Messrs. Nayler and Marks put themselves in evidence; in which case what would become of the round-robin? the only effect of whose previous existence would be to weaken the personal claim of the two gentlemen in question upon Mr. Peyton's gratitude. These arguments were unanswerable, or, rather, the only answer which Messrs. Nayler and Marks had to offer—namely, that any course seemed preferable to them to taking the whole risk of the enterprise on their own shoulders—it was forbidden them to use. They had gone too far to retreat or retract; and indeed, when on one occasion Mr. Marks exhibited most unquestionable signs of jibbing, Mr. Ralph Dornay had taken him to task with a very high hand, and expressed his opinion that it was incredible that a man of his intellectual status could be so deficient in common honesty as to allow his friend and patron to be imposed upon, when he had the information in his own hands which could prevent it. And when Mr. Nayler eagerly corroborated this view of affairs with his 'Very true,' Mr. Dornay turned on him with no little indignation, and observed that what he had been compelled to say to Mr. Marks was equally applicable to Mr. Nayler. Nevertheless the disinclination of both these gentlemen to bell the cat was so extreme that, in spite of their backers' expectations, they positively declined to appeal to Mr. Beryl Peyton in person, but set down what they had to say in an epistle marked 'Private,' and to which their respective signatures were affixed in a handwriting which was the reverse of ' bold.'

The fact was that, however Mr. Beryl Peyton was admired and revered by the members of the Happy Family (concerning which none who heard them speak of him could surely entertain a doubt), there was not one who was not secretly afraid of him, and especially of those bursts of passion in which (in common with less benevolent ' Deputy Providences,' such as Peter the Great) he was occasionally accustomed to indulge.

CHAPTER XLIV.

PULLING THE TRIGGER.

It was one of the privileges of those who from time to time Mr. Beryl Peyton placed in the forefront of his favours, to be admitted into his counsels, and to have their advice demanded upon this or that scheme of benevolence; a circumstance which sometimes proved the cause of their undoing.

'First catch your patron,' may be an important proviso, but it is useless unless you possess the art of keeping him: and this is the more difficult the more familiar you are with him, inasmuch as he has thereby opportunities to find out how much he was mistaken in you. And thus it had happened to more than one whom Mr. Beryl Peyton had delighted to honour. They had been created grand viziers, only to be bowstrung, or at all events to be banished from their master's presence, and to have their names obliterated from his will.

Up to this time Edgar Dornay had held his place by the throne without misadventure: partly perhaps because he did not take such pains to keep it as some of his predecessors had done. He was not blind to his own interests, and, as we know, by no means disinclined to the possession of great wealth; but he was not one of those who think that gold can never be bought too dearly, or who have a natural hunger for it. He was neither grasping nor greedy, and much too fond of his ease to seek wealth at the sacrifice of comfort. His manners were agreeable without sycophancy. To Beryl Peyton, who was accustomed to the fulsome arts of expectation, it appeared that the young man had both independence and self-respect. He had never fallen into the error

of making stepping-stones of others into Mr.
Peyton's favour, nor fomented his anger against
them; and his behaviour as Mary Marvon's
rejected suitor had been unexceptionable.
He had accepted his *congé* with such good
humour that Mr. Peyton, who was of course
in ignorance of his previous love-passages with
Mary, had complimented him upon it.

' Well, sir, of course I am disappointed,'
Edgar had said, ' and the more so because I
see you are disappointed too. It would have
been easy to shrug my shoulders—impertinence is always easy—but there is no reason,
because Miss Marvon refuses me her love,
that I should cease to respect her. For my
part, I think it a piece of great arrogance to
cut the throat of a young lady (as I read in
the newspapers often happens) simply because
one has failed to recommend oneself to her.
That dog-in-the-manger notion of " If I can't
have her nobody else shall " seems to me, to
say no worse of it, both egotistic and con-
temptible.'

These generous sentiments were very agreeable to Mr. Beryl Peyton, but he had discovered expectation in so many garbs that he was not quite certain of their genuineness. An opportunity now arose to test it.

There came a certain day when to an attentive observer the dinner party at the Hall seemed to have a cloud upon it.

Mr. Charles Sotheran indeed was not aware of its existence: and if he had been, it would scarcely have attracted his attention. He was as independent of clouds as a man in a waterproof, or rather there was a reflected sunshine about him (emanating from his next neighbour) which destroyed their influence. He had understood from Mr. Rennie (still specially retained on the premises) that when he returned to town to resume his duties at the Probate Office, it was within the bounds of possibility that he should take Mary with him; and this naturally afforded him an agreeable topic of conversation with his proposed fellow-traveller.

Except that Mary looked forward with unfeigned regret to her parting from her hostess, no two young people were ever more thoroughly happy. It must be added, to their honour, that all the ladies sympathised with them; even Miss Price, who had never been wooed, and Mrs. Welbeck, who had been wooed once too often. It is the attribute of all women, not naturally bad, or soured by disappointment, to feel a kindly interest in turtle-doves about to mate. Their coo finds a responsive echo in their gentle breasts as surely as does that of a baby. As for Mrs. Peyton, her pleasure in the contemplation of the happiness of her young favourites made her almost oblivious of the vacancy their absence would create in her heart and home. Could she see them married, she could certainly die happy; and as to living, the time for that she was well convinced would be but short. If gloom intruded upon her, it was cast by the dread of delay. As the time drew near for the accomplishment of her

hopes, the least incident excited her fears;
and it did not escape her notice that certain
of her guests were more silent than usual,
and seemed to avoid even exchanging glances
with one another.   Had she watched them
more narrowly, she might have observed that
Mr. Ralph Dornay's manner was more frank
and *débonnaire* than was usual with him
since he had come into his wife's property,
and that more than once Dr. Bilde conde-
scended to exchange a few words with him
in his superior manner upon unimportant
subjects.   It seemed as though, freed for
a while from their respective responsibilities,
these representatives of science and social
position had agreed to unbend, and even that
they made some point of impressing upon
society that for the moment they had nothing
of supreme importance upon their minds.
Mr. Marks and Mr. Nayler, on the contrary,
preserved an unbroken silence, and kept their
eyes fixed upon their plates, save that now
and then they snatched a furtive glance in

the direction of Mr. Beryl Peyton, who was dispensing hospitality in his matter-of-course manner, and conversing with Edgar Dornay about the window-gardens of the poor.

Of the proverbial bad quarter of an hour after dinner, the two philosophers had little experience: they had not settled many dinner bills, but they endured quite enough on the present occasion to restore the average. Over the dessert, when the ladies had withdrawn, they suffered agonies of suspense and apprehension. For though the bill of indictment that had been formed against Charles Sotheran and Mary Marvon had been placed that morning, with their names affixed to it, in Mr. Peyton's hands, he had not even acknowledged its receipt. The pistol which had been so skilfully loaded for them they had let off with their own hands, yet no report had followed. Had it missed fire altogether, or what? In that 'what' lay the most terrible contingencies. Was it Mr. Peyton's intention to treat the matter with silent contempt, or

to visit them with his wrath and indignation?
Or was he only making inquiries into the
truth of their allegations before proceeding
to action?   Had he taken that operation of
having his eyes opened in the very worst
part, he could hardly have hit upon a form
of punishment more severe than that which
he was at present inflicting.

It by no means mitigated their apprehensions that, when they applied to Dr. Bilde in
their extremity, he gave them neither encouragement nor comfort; nay, what seemed
monstrous in a person of his profession, he
had not even advice to offer them.   He only
remarked that to a well-regulated mind the
approval of one's own conscience, and the
conviction that we have done our best to
further the cause of moral order, should be
a sufficient compensation for whatever happens.

As for Mr. Ralph Dornay, he merely
shrugged his shoulders and smiled, as a man
with thirty thousand a year can afford to

smile at the pecuniary perplexities of his fellow-creatures.

‘When you go in for a great stake,
gentlemen,’ he said, with his thumbs in the
armholes of his waistcoat, ‘ it is only reasonable that you should incur some risk.’

To the observation that he had put the
thing into their heads, he replied that to reveal what gentlemen said to one another in
casual conversation was a breach of confidence, and that to make any use of it to
his disadvantage was held on all hands to be
so dishonourable that the injured person was
justified in giving a distinct denial to anything
and everything. This was said with the air
of a man who intends to act up to his
principles.

Even on a bed of down we are told
that conscience is uneasy. But still one is
unwilling to exchange it for a wool mattress:
and each of the two philosophers passed a
wretched night, from the reflection that it
might possibly be the very last time that

(left to his own resources) he would sleep in a feather bed.

In Mr. Peyton's study after breakfast some 'private theatricals' took place of rather a serious kind. As Edgar and his host were smoking their cigars together as usual, the elder gentleman threw an open letter over to his companion, with a dry 'Read that.' It was a missive of great length, and had not come by the post, but had been placed in Mr. Peyton's hands by his valet, 'With Mr. Nayler's compliments,' on the previous morning. It took some minutes to get through it, and even when it was done Edgar remained speechless, but full of thought. It is possible that he was hesitating between honour and self-interest: if so, it was fortunate for him that he decided in favour of the former, since if he had taken the course which looked most to his own advantage he would have repented it.

There were several of the Happy Family for trial that morning, and among them (to judge by the way in which Mr. Peyton looked at him from under his large white hand) was Edgar Dornay himself.

'Well, what do you think of it, Dornay?'

'They are lying, sir,' was the quiet reply.

'You mean as regards the girl? You think it impossible——'

'I do not think, because I am quite certain,' put in Edgar, vehemently, 'that Miss Marvon has done nothing to be ashamed of.'

'But perhaps—long ago,' suggested the old man, tenderly, 'under circumstances at which we cannot guess, harassed by trouble, pinched by poverty, tempted—who can tell?'

'*I* can tell,' answered Edgar, quietly. 'Never, never.'

Mr. Peyton hid his eyes, for they sparkled with pleasure.

'But the lad,' he went on; 'it looks bad against the lad.'

'They have made it look bad,' said Edgar.

His tone had changed; it was still confident, but had lost its fervour. The matter was comparatively indifferent to him. On the other hand, the man was his successful rival, and it therefore behoved him (an idea which, though they were so full of ideas, would never have occurred to Mr. Marks or Mr. Nayler) to say what good he knew of him.

'Still, if he said these things,' said Mr. Peyton, pointing to the letter, ' it was most ungrateful, and I hate ingratitude.'

' Mr. Sotheran's nature is not, in my opinion, an ungrateful one. I will even say '—this with a dead lift, but he did say it—' that it is incapable of ingratitude.'

· They say he called me Tarquinius Superbus,' muttered Mr. Peyton, pulling at his long white beard.

'I did not say that Mr. Sotheran was incapable of an impertinence,' was the quiet reply.

' These gentlemen, to use their own words,' said Mr. Peyton, 'have " courted investigation." I have caused certain inquiries to be made, the result of which will be placed before us. They have asked for justice ; they shall have it. Will you oblige me by ringing the bell ? '

CHAPTER XLV.

THE INDICTMENT.

EDGAR DORNAY was very far from wishing to be a spectator of what was about to follow. But an heir presumptive has his duties, and it was a part of them in this case to stand on the right hand of the sovereign while administering justice. In the Letcombe Dottrell kingdom there was a still more significant sign of heirship—namely, to be present during Mr. Peyton's confidences with his lawyer; but to that topmost peak of expectation Edgar Dornay had not yet reached. Though on a very high rung of the ladder, he was still on his promotion. Mr. Peyton had never to ring twice except for a reason: when he did so, it produced not the footman but his valet.

'Derwood,' he said, 'ask Mr. Marks and Mr. Nayler to be so good as to favour me with their company.'

Nothing could be more stolidly respectful than Mr. Derwood's face as he left the room to execute his master's orders, but directly the door had closed behind him it became full of expression. Sailors talk in their melodramatic manner of 'the plank between them and eternity,' but a great man's door is also a plank of some importance, on one side of which things take place that never occur upon the other.

'Here 's another row,' soliloquised the valet, laying his finger to the side of his nose, as was his habit when reflecting upon the changes and chances of human life, of which, since he had been some years at Letcombe Hall, he had seen something: 'if the goose of them two gents isn't cooked, my name isn't Sam Derwood.' Then, as if suddenly affected by a reminiscence (though, in his case, it was the absence of one), he added briskly, 'and a

good job too. I don't remember as either
of them ever gave me so much as would buy
a cigar with.'

If there is a mammon of unrighteousness
which it behoves persons who live in expectancy
to make friends of, it is their patron's valet;
yet Messrs. Marks and Nayler had entirely
omitted this precaution. They ought by rights
to have been millionaires, so slow they were to
part with their money. Mr. Marks, it is true,
had fee'd Scarsdale, because her evidence was
important to the present inquiry, and Mr.
Nayler (not to waste his means upon a mere
presentment) had chucked her under the chin;
but the bribe in neither case would have been
sufficient to enlist her aid had she not been
disposed to help them for other reasons. Now,
though years of service had robbed Scarsdale
of her youth, they had enabled her (in compensation) to put by a tidy sum of money,
whereof Mr. Samuel Derwood being enamoured,
he had proposed to her; and, either in order
to make a cheap show of virtue, or to stimu-

late Mr. Derwood himself to similar gallantries, she had confessed in her own way (she had even added 'he kissed me') Mr. Nayler's indiscretion to the valet.

His jealous indignation may be imagined. 'What!' he cried, 'do you mean to say he never gave you nothing to take the taste out of it? Scaly varmint!'

Ignorant of this extraneous enemy, but with sufficient apprehensions of danger from more direct sources, the two philosophers were ushered into the hall of audience. Mr. Peyton, standing with his back to the fireplace, gravely pointed out two chairs immediately opposite that in which his young friend was already seated. Never had involuntary spectator a better view of any performance than the unfortunate Edgar.

'I have requested my friend Mr. Dornay's presence here,' observed Mr. Peyton in explanation, 'because I have confidence in his judgment, and also because he has some knowledge of the previous history of the two persons whom the document you have placed in my hands concerns. He is already acquainted with its contents, so that it will be unnecessary to read it. Have you anything to add, gentlemen, to the information which it purports to afford?'

'Nothing, save that it is all true,' observed Mr. Marks, in a solemn tone. It had been agreed between the two accusers that Mr. Marks should be their mouthpiece, and if he had been appointed Speaker to the House of Commons he could not have acquitted himself with greater dignity and sedateness.

'That is a bold thing to say of eight pages of manuscript,' returned Mr. Peyton; 'yet even if it *were* true, I should have thought you might at least have added that it was with sincere regret you found yourself compelled to make such allegations against two young people whose future fortunes it was only too likely to affect for ill. But perhaps,' he added, with unmistakable irony, 'you never thought of the future.'

This was very rough on the philosophers, whose silence (which had provoked this outbreak) was in reality caused by the embarrassment of their position. What Mr. Marks had had it on the tip of his tongue to say was that it was with a bleeding heart he had forced himself to make these charges, but that, where the interests of so dear and revered a friend as Mr. Beryl Peyton were concerned, all other considerations sank into insignificance. But such sentiments are for a patron's ear alone. With Edgar Dornay sitting within two feet of him, it was really impossible to indulge in them. Far from suspecting that that gentleman was almost as uncomfortable as himself, he did him the injustice of supposing him capable of exclaiming 'Rubbish!' at the conclusion of some burst of loyalty.

Mr. Marks did, however, manage to say that he had only performed what was to him a most unpleasant duty. He had noticed that Mr. Peyton had showed considerable favour to Mr. Charles Sotheran; and the gross ingratitude which the young man had evinced when speaking of his benefactor, not to mention the motives of self-interest by which he was evidently actuated——"

'Never mind the motives,' interrupted Mr. Peyton, drily. 'We can all supply those for one another. Let us stick to facts. He was disrespectful to me in his conversation, it seems?'

'Very,' observed Mr. Marks.

'And frequently, eh?'

'Always,' struck in Mr. Nayler.

'Then it strikes me you must have encouraged him,' suggested Mr. Peyton.

Nothing, averred both gentlemen, could be more groundless than such an accusation. They had been too appalled to stop him, and simply let him run on. What must have been their feelings, for example, Mr. Marks ventured to inquire, with a glance towards the indictment— what must have been their righteous indignation when this young person had the audacity to liken his patron to Tarquinius Superbus?

'Why did he call me that, I wonder?' inquired Mr. Peyton, with a glance at Edgar.

> ' Though white as Mount Soracte
> When winter nights are long,'

suggested the young poet,

> ' His beard flowed down o'er mail and belt,
> His heart and hand were strong.'

'To be sure—a very apt quotation,' observed the old man, smiling. 'His other remarks, however, it seems were not so complimentary. Is this allegation literally true, gentlemen, that Mr. Sotheran said "The old fool"' (he here read an extract from the indictment) ' "will settle some money on the girl (meaning Miss Marvon), and then I will marry her:" and again, "I wish the old fool was dead"?'

'Those were the words Mr. Sotheran used,' said Mr. Marks, with a slight cough, as if something stuck in his throat.

'Is that your impression also, Mr. Nayler?'

'He made use, if not of those actual words, of words of a similar purport, sir.'

'There was a witness once who said "the prisoner cried 'Bill, Bill,' *or words to that effect,*"' observed Mr. Peyton, drily. 'I trust, Mr. Nayler, you will be found to be equally conscientious. I have made inquiries, however, into this matter, and testimony will be produced which does not quite bear out what you two gentlemen have said. It tends to prove, I am sorry to say, that though Mr. Sotheran may have been indiscreet and disrespectful in his language, a certain colour has been given to it.'

'Not by us, sir,' murmured Mr. Marks. A dreadful suspicion crossed his mind that Ralph Dornay and Dr. Bilde were acting treacherously to them, and for some reason of their own had turned informers. For to what other testimony could their host refer?

Mr. Peyton rang the bell, and by some intermediate agency—for it is certain he could never have heard it—it was answered by Japhet Marcom, the deaf mute.

Notwithstanding his height and strong build, this man had usually the patient, apathetic look which belongs to those who are similarly afflicted—a gentle attentiveness, as if they would fain listen to you if they could. But on this occasion there was a severity in his face that almost approached truculence.

'You have seen these gentlemen walking on the terrace lately now and then, Japhet,' said Mr. Peyton, indicating the two philosophers with his finger.

Japhet's eyes shone 'yes,' as he inclined his head with quiet confidence.

' And from where you were you could hear —in your way—pretty accurately what they said ?'

Mr. Marks and Mr. Nayler smiled incredulously, as indeed did Edgar himself. Japhet's services were devoted to his master, and not given to the public at large. If the Happy Family ever bestowed a thought upon him, it was to conclude (as indeed was the fact) that his name was to be found among the lesser blessed in Mr. Peyton's will. They knew that his master and he had some mysterious means of communicating with one another, and that was all.

'You seem to doubt Japhet's powers, gentlemen,' observed Mr. Peyton. 'Be so kind, Mr. Dornay, as to ask him a question for yourself.'

'Is the clock at the church, Japhet,' inquired Edgar, 'faster or slower than the Hall time?'

The mute pointed to the timepiece over the mantelpiece, and moved his hand with great rapidity.

'He says our time is faster,' explained Mr. Peyton. 'If you had made the inquiry fifty feet hence, and in a whisper, he would have heard you equally well. If he is near enough to see the movement of your lips, he can tell what they say. If you doubt this, gentlemen, you can make proof of it for yourselves, but for my part I know it to be the case; and whatever Japhet has repeated to me of this matter is, to my mind, I frankly tell you, testimony to be relied on as surely as though he had made a third at your interviews, and every word you said had been addressed to him.'

Mr. Marks's lips moved as if he himself were dumb; Mr. Nayler gibbered like a ghost or a detected presentment.

'Japhet has, at my suggestion,' continued Mr. Peyton, 'written out a detailed account of what he heard in the walled garden. It is here, open to your inspection, gentlemen, and —if it can be refuted—to your refutation. Japhet alleges that you agreed together that there could be no harm in putting into Mr. Sotheran's mouth the sentiments which you took it for granted he entertained. For example, since you supposed he would like Miss Marvon no less for being well dowered, you thought it a natural thing to make Mr. Sotheran say, "The old fool will settle some

money on the girl, and then I will marry her."
Do you still maintain, gentlemen, that those
were the actual words Mr. Sotheran used?
On the other hand, Japhet is confident as to
your own employment of this rather singular
phrase'—here Mr. Peyton once more referred
to the manuscript—' " By hook or by crook, we
must get both the boy and the wench out of
the house." '

'It seems to me, Mr. Peyton,' said Mr.
Marks, turning very pale and speaking in
quavering tones, ' that you have hardly behaved
quite fairly to us in discussing in the presence
of a third person '—here he indicated Edgar
Dornay—' a matter which was communicated
to you under the seal of confidence. Our
communication, if you will be so good as to
observe, was marked " private and confidential." '

'Good heavens, sir! am I the Lion of
Venice,' exclaimed Mr. Peyton, angrily, ' that
I should take every charge for granted that
malice and ill-will may invent against an

innocent man? If I hesitate to confront him with his accusers, do you suppose that it is for their sakes, and merely because they have expressed a wish—under the circumstances, a very natural wish—to remain anonymous? What right have you to complain because I take this gentleman here into my confidence? What hinders you from defending yourselves because he is present?'

It was rather difficult for poor Mr. Marks to explain his position; the statement that his conversations with Mr. Nayler had been over-heard, which he did not in the least doubt, had utterly overwhelmed him. He was con-scious of having said so many damaging things. There seemed to him but one way of escape for them out of the hole, just as the fox made use of the goat in the well, namely, on the shoulders of Mr. Ralph Dornay. He would like to have said that the character that gentleman had given them of Mr. Sotheran had so utterly shocked their sense of pro-priety that they had taken what might certainly seem somewhat extreme measures to prevent Mr. Peyton's favour from being abused. They had gone, perhaps, further than they were justified in going, but not of themselves—Mr. Ralph Dornay had given them the momentum. This is what seemed their best and, indeed, their only line of defence; but how could they take it in the presence of Mr. Dornay's nephew?

'You must remember, sir,' said Mr. Marks, wetting his dry lips as the serpent flickers with his forked tongue, 'that there is another person implicated in this unhappy matter, and that a motive of delicacy, which you will, I am sure, both understand and appreciate, prevents its full discussion—ahem!—under present circumstances.'

'Pray do not let your consideration for Miss Marvon stand in your way,' replied Mr. Peyton, coldly. 'If you have nothing more to say against the young lady than you have had to urge against Mr. Sotheran, it will not distress Mr. Dornay, though he entertains as high a regard for her as any one must do who has the good fortune to be acquainted with her.'

'You must please to remember, Mr. Peyton,' said Mr. Marks, hurriedly, ' that we have personally made no charge of any kind against Miss Marvon. We have only repeated, from a sense of what was owing to yourself, what we have heard of her from other sources, and which a very little inquiry on your part will corroborate or disprove.'

'You speak of other sources,' said Mr. Peyton, icily: 'be so good as to name one of them.'

'Permit me, sir, to mention Scarsdale, Mrs. Peyton's maid.'

CHAPTER XLVI.

SCARSDALE'S TESTIMONY.

AT the name of Mrs. Peyton there flitted across her husband's face an angry flush. Notwithstanding his democratic opinions, and the freedom with which he mingled with his inferiors, Beryl Peyton was intensely proud, though, as men of his class often are, only at second hand. He himself, that is, had no objection to be treated as an equal by any human being; but his belongings were 'taboo.' He resented—and all the more because he himself paid so little deference to her opinions—the least disrespect shown to his wife. Even the introduction of her maid's name into the matter on hand annoyed him, because it might be the prelude to the citation

of Mrs. Peyton herself. Nevertheless, he was
not the man to suffer his private feelings to
interfere with the course of justice.

'If Mrs. Peyton's maid has anything to say
to this matter, let her say it,' he said, and that
lady was summoned accordingly.

To Messrs. Marks and Nayler her appearance gave a great relief, for they felt that in
her hands their cause was far safer than in
their own. As a junior, with the conduct of a
great case unexpectedly thrust upon his inade-
quate shoulders, joys to see his leader suddenly
appear in court, and trusts that his mistakes
will be repaired and his lost ground recovered,
so did they hail the appearance of their
female ally. Though very far from being
innocents, they were ill adapted by nature for
plots and stratagems; and if they had not
known as much half an hour ago, they knew
it now. They were conscious of having, so
far, made a complete and deplorable failure of
the little matter they had taken in hand. On
paper—that is to say, while they were talking

the affair over between themselves—their plan of the campaign had seemed to be perfect. Each had only to corroborate the other's story, and the thing was done. That the cause should ever come to be tried in open court had never entered into their calculations. It was shameful that such doubts should have been thrown upon two gentlemen's words, while as for the unlooked-for intervention of Japhet Marcom, it was a circumstance little short of diabolic. But what in reality more alarmed them and put them off their balance than all the rest was the tone and manner of Mr. Peyton himself. What they had looked for was not indeed an upright judge : they had imagined that, weighed down by the sense of obligation arising from their disinterested action, he would have leant very considerably in their direction ; whereas it was now evident that he was inclining to the other side.

Hitherto, however, testimony had been hostile to them : in the excellent Scarsdale they felt sure of a partisan. She had spoken to them of Miss Marvon with such bitterness upon her own account that they were confident nothing would be wanting to her accuracy in the way of zeal. She was not beautiful, but they did not require a Phryne to plead their cause. Her high colour suggested animus— the right animus; her set lips resolution; nor did her large black eyes abate their keenness one whit, though she stood in the presence of her master.

'You have something to say, it seems, concerning Miss Marvon,' observed Mr. Peyton, quietly. 'What is it?'

'About Miss Marvon? Me, sir? No, sir!'

Her look was innocence itself, mingled with amazed surprise.

'Well, you *have* said something about her, at all events,' said Mr. Peyton, coldly. 'Is it not so, gentlemen?' He addressed his remarks to the two philosophers, but Scarsdale answered it.

'Not as I am aware on, sir. I have never

spoken of the young lady except in answer to questions.'

If this reply was accidental it was a most unfortunate one for the prosecutors, since it suggested the process called pumping; but if it was intentional—designed, that is, to isolate them and place the speaker herself in a position of neutrality—their case was pitiable indeed. Mr. Marks felt like an indifferent swimmer, who, having just seized hold of some sapling on the bank which promised safety, finds it gradually coming up by the roots.

'Mr. Nayler and I put certain inquiries to this young person,' he explained, 'which were necessitated by the circumstances of the case. We knew that there was a secret—I regret to say a shameful secret—connected with Miss Marvon's past, and we thought, acting as we were in your interests, that the most likely person to enlighten us upon the subject was her waiting maid.'

'I am not Miss Marvon's maid,' exclaimed Scarsdale, vehemently.

To a close observer this was the first sign of naturalness which this lady had evinced: hitherto she had been under the influence of a severe self-restraint, but in these words she broke away from it.

'Of course not, Scarsdale,' put in Mr. Marks, soothingly: 'you are Mrs. Peyton's own maid; still, you have necessarily seen much of her companion. Now, what did you tell me and Mr. Nayler here, on Wednesday last, respecting her?'

'Nothing; nothing, that is, as I particularly remember.'

'Oh dear, oh dear! but you surely must,' insisted Mr. Marks. The fact of his having given her half a sovereign on the occasion in question had impressed all the surrounding circumstances so vividly upon his own mind that he could not understand this plea of forgetfulness in another. 'You told us, you know, how very intimate your mistress was with Miss Marvon, so much so that it made the young lady "forget her place," as you expressed it.'

'I don't remember,' reiterated Scarsdale, stolidly. This second dislaimer was a mistake: it is possible to make a false step in refusing to take any step at all. It was clear to both Mr. Peyton and to Edgar that the phrase in question had been Scarsdale's own. This seemed even to strike herself—or perhaps the glances they exchanged with each other did not escape her —for she presently added, 'I don't say as missis and Miss Marvon were not intimate.'

'Just so, and very confidential,' put in Mr. Marks. 'They talked together pretty often of Miss Marvon's proposed marriage, did they not?'

'Sometimes.'

'And your mistress seemed to be in a hurry about it, did she not? Now, why was that?'

'Because,' said Scarsdale, slowly, and with her eyes on the carpet, 'missis felt far from well, and seemed afraid she should never live to see the marriage in which she took such an interest take place.'

'Will you swear,' inquired Mr. Marks, with

indignation, 'that the reason you gave to me wasn't that there was something discreditable about Miss Marvon which time might bring to light, and that therefore she was in a hurry to get the matter concluded, with Mr. Peyton's sanction?'

Scarsdale looked up to the ceiling, and half opened her mouth (as though to depict or allegorise an effort of memory), then shook her head and answered rapidly, like a gentleman used to taking official affidavits, 'No, I never did!'

'Then perhaps you will also venture to affirm,' said Mr. Marks, with the calmness of despair, 'that you did not quote to me the other day, "This house for you is full of pitfalls," as an expression used by Mrs. Peyton to Miss Marvon to denote the imminent danger of her secret being discovered so long as she remained at Letcombe Hall?'

Miss Scarsdale's colour heightened, she cast at her master a furtive inquiring glance, as though she would have asked, 'Now what do *you* think? If I said "I didn't," should I pass the extreme limit of that credulity a gentleman owes to a lady's word or not?' Then boldly answered, 'No; I don't remember nothing about pitfalls.'

It was an audacious stroke, but it failed. I sympathise with her, because when I myself have a story suggested to me I never can tell it like one for which I am indebted to my own fancy; and Miss Scarsdale was acting under instructions. Her instinct was to tell the truth and more. She would have liked to have said all she knew of Miss Marvon, and have added to it what she thought of her. But Mr. Derwood had forbidden it. It might be thought, since she was ten years his senior, that she ought to have known best how to act, but his youth—or comparative youth—was the very thing that gave him so much influence with her. It was probably her last chance of a husband. 'The game is up, Maria,' he had said. 'I can see by the governor's look that them two gents are in Queer Street; so whatever you do, say nothing to back 'em.' And this had been the secret of Scarsdale's tergiversation—as simple as Columbus's egg trick, when you came to know it, but to Mr. Marks and Mr. Nayler, who didn't know it, utterly inexplicable. It is no wonder she had not acted naturally the rôle thus imposed on her. Who could expect the villain of a piece to take a virtuous part at a moment's notice, and play it with any gusto? At those words, 'I don't remember nothing about pitfalls,' Mr. Peyton leant across to Edgar, and, without taking much pains to drop his voice, observed, 'This woman is lying.'

Poor Scarsdale! Left to herself she might have scrambled on along the way of villainy for life with considerable success, till she came to the precipice whither we must all come, but this solitary attempt to tread the path of virtue (though it was altogether involuntary) was her ruin. She had the misfortune to be afflicted with the malady (not solely confined to females) called a 'temper.' Blind with wrath, oblivious of her betrothed and his injunctions, and utterly careless of consistency, she hastened to retrace her steps.

'If you don't believe me, and want to hear something as 'll make your hair stand on end, you had better ask Miss Marvon herself.'

'A very good plan,' observed Mr. Peyton, in cold and measured tones. He might have been a statue carved in granite, but that at the same moment he nodded significantly to Japhet Marcom. It was not a moment too soon. As the deaf mute stepped forward to put the furious woman out of the room, she broke out—

'Miss Marvon, indeed! You want to know about her, do you? Ask Mr. Ralph Dornay; ask Dr. Bilde; ask Miss Innocence herself. Hoity, toity! here 's a fuss about a pretty face. There 's no fool like an——'

The rest of the proverb was lost in the passage, but the application of it was preserved by the contemptuous glance she cast, before the door closed on her ejected form, at Mr. Beryl Peyton.

CHAPTER XLVII.

SUSPICION.

EARNESTNESS has become so common a trade, and also so mechanical a one, that the expression of it has little effect on anybody. A touch of nature, on the other hand (which nowadays one meets with but seldom), goes home to every heart. Miss Scarsdale might not have been right in the opinion she had expressed, or hinted, with respect to Miss Mary Marvon, but it had been obviously a genuine one, and so far had its merits. It may seem strange that the wild words of an angry waiting-woman should so move a man like Beryl Peyton, but the truth was, that parting shot of hers, ' Ask Mr. Ralph Dornay, ask Dr. Bilde, ask Miss Innocence herself,' had pierced his very heart. It had suggested—what is feared almost as much by the patron as by the tyrant—a conspiracy. To a benevolent man who has any knowledge of the world, ingratitude in the individual is nothing surprising. It is one of the drawbacks to which the profession of philanthropy is naturally exposed, as that of the farmer is to a bad harvest, or that of the merchant to a bad debt; but when the objects of one's benevolence band together, and conspire to hoodwink us, the matter becomes serious, because it implies something amiss in our private compensation balance for setting the world to rights—something rotten at the root of our own system. If Mr. Ralph Dornay and Dr. Bilde knew something discreditable about Mary Marvon, and had suffered him, thought Beryl Peyton, to waste his favours, and, what was worse, his affection, upon an unworthy object, why might not others know it? It was true they had shown no liking for her, but even that might have been a part of their duplicity: they might have been in league together none the less that they showed no sign of alliance. On the other hand, he was very unwilling to believe anything to Mary's discredit. Her sweetness of disposition had won upon him further than he cared to acknowledge, and also in spite of himself. Once before he had been moved very strongly in favour of a young girl, in a somewhat similar position in that very house, and she had disappointed him cruelly. She had listened to the unworthy solicitations of his own son, which had proved the beginning of unutterable troubles. Was it possible that he was about to be disappointed and deceived a second time? While these bitter thoughts were falling through his mind like sleet, Mr. Nayler spoke. Up to this time, and while matters had been going so dead against him, that gentleman had been well content to use Mr. Marks for a mouthpiece, but now that things had taken a decided turn in his favour he was moved to speak, as a bird tunes his note in the sunshine after showers.

'You were saying it would be a good plan,

Mr. Peyton, to question Miss Marvon herself. That strikes me as an excellent suggestion.'

Whether excellent or not, it was certainly not an original one, for it had been proposed by Miss Scarsdale. And this consideration, among others, may have made it unwelcome to Mr. Peyton.

'Do you suppose I am going to send for the young lady *here*,' he exclaimed with indignation, 'to be examined and cross-examined by you and Mr. Marks? Or even that I should expose her to the indignity of answering questions of a private nature in your presence?'

'Certainly not, sir,' said Mr. Nayler, hurriedly. To do him justice, he would have shrunk from any such proceeding: what he would have preferred was to have been an unseen spectator of the investigation—like Lady Teazle in the screen scene, only more virtuous —and to have disclosed himself at the *dénouement*, just as Mary was being turned out of the house.

'Then, I think, gentlemen,' said Mr. Peyton, 'you had better withdraw. You may be assured of justice being done in this affair in your absence, just as though you were witnesses to its administration.'

'We leave the matter in your hands, sir,' said Mr. Marks, rising, 'with the utmost confidence in your sense of right; and whatever may come of this investigation—the necessity for which we deeply deplore—we feel assured that you will give us credit at least for having had no other end in view than the exposure of unworthiness.'

'I do not pretend to be a judge of motives, Mr. Marks,' was the dry reply; 'but the facts of the case, you may rely upon it, shall be thoroughly investigated.' Mr. Nayler drew out his handkerchief—Mr. Marks had a dreadful misgiving that he was about to burst into tears and confess all—and wiped the perspiration from his forehead. If it was a device to gain time, in order to say a word or two on his own account after the other had left the room, it failed of its intent. Mr. Marks slipped his arm within his own, and led him out like a lady, but with a certain amount of vigour that forbade delay.

Thus left alone with his young friend, Mr. Peyton turned towards him with a grave, pained face.

'What do you think of it all, Mr. Dornay?' he inquired.

'As respects Miss Marvon, sir, my opinion is quite unaltered.'

'I am glad to hear you say so. Still there is some scandal afoot regarding her, which it is necessary for her own sake to get to the bottom of. That woman we have just seen believed it: those gentlemen believed it.'

'Let us say they wished to believe it, sir.'

'Perhaps; I am not sure,' returned the other, gravely. 'We must give no verdict till we have heard all the evidence.'

'It is quite impossible, however,' said Edgar, apprehensively, 'as you were saying, to interrogate Miss Marvon herself;' and indeed it is but fair to say that Edgar Dornay would have

given up all his hopes of inheritance to Beryl
Peyton's wealth (though he knew them by this
time to be well founded) rather than have been
a party to any such thing.

'Quite true; but I must learn the truth,
and the whole truth,' said the old man. 'There
is something wrong. " Pitfalls," he murmured;
" this place," she said, " is full of pitfalls."
Rennie knows her; I will ask Rennie to speak
with her. I wish I had spoken to Rennie at
first.'

To one who knew Beryl Peyton this admission of a mistake in the presence of another
person was full of significance, and augured
well indeed for the fortunes of his confidant.
The Catholic religion was one that would never
have attracted him to its fold, since it enjoins
the confession of errors: not even to himself,
when anything went wrong, was Mr. Peyton
accustomed to own that it had done so through
his own fault.

'At all events there has been no harm
done,' said Edgar, soothingly. This was taking

a sanguine view of affairs; for two philosophers, a serving-man that is neither deaf nor dumb, and an angry waiting-maid, with a suspected but undiscovered secret amongst them, are surely elements of disturbance in any household. Reading something of this in Mr. Peyton's face as he laid his hand upon the bellrope, 'Don't you think,' continued Edgar, 'that instead of sending for Mr. Rennie, it will be well for me to go and fetch him? You could then consult together on what would be advisable, without attracting public attention.'

'Right, my lad, as you usually are,' said Mr. Peyton, approvingly. 'You will find him in his room, no doubt. Just ask him to step round.'

Mr. Edgar Dornay's advice had been even more discreet than his host had imagined it to be. In offering it he had had his own enfranchisement in view at least as much as anything else, and when Mr. Rennie, after some interval, made his appearance, he was alone.

' Where is Edgar? ' were Mr. Peyton's first words.

' Gone for a constitutional—at least, so he said.'

' Ah, that was his excuse : he did not wish to intrude his presence without an express invitation. What I like him for is his delicacy.'

' Perhaps it was that which made him feel the atmosphere of the court a little oppressive,' said the lawyer, drily. ' He seemed uncommonly glad to get away.'

' The whole proceedings were very painful to him, no doubt,' assented Mr. Peyton. ' I take it for granted he has told you what has passed.'

The lawyer nodded gravely.

' His own behaviour throughout has been most admirable,' continued Mr. Peyton, earnestly.

' He told me that too,' said the lawyer ; ' or at least led me to conclude as much.'

' You are very hard and very unjust, as you always are, in the case of every one in whom I take an interest,' said Mr. Peyton, walking to and fro and speaking with great irritation.

'It's such a waste of sympathy to take your first view of them,' said Mr. Rennie, 'since in the end you always find them out.'

'In Edgar Dornay there is nothing to find out,' observed the other, confidently.

'At all events he isn't the subject of our present discussion,' answered the lawyer, drily 'You wish to speak to me, as I understand, about Miss Marvon.'

'Yes ; Marks and Nayler have put *this* into my hands—a sort of bill of indictment; and here's Japhet's account of the matter, which puts a part of it—that which relates to Sotheran—in a very different point of view. Just run your eye over them.'

When the lawyer had finished this exami- nation he looked up and observed quietly, 'The thing's plain enough in my judgment. It is not the first time, my dear Peyton, nor the second, that you have asked my opinion upon a similar set of circumstances.'

'You think it 's mere jealousy—the wish to supplant?'

'How can you doubt it? " By hook or by crook we must get the boy and wench out of the house" is the key to the whole position. Japhet is sure about the words, I conclude.'

'Quite certain. But both Marks and Nayler assert most positively that there is something in the girl's past of which she has reason to be ashamed.'

'Who told them that?' inquired Mr. Rennie, quickly.

'I don't know. Marks said "other sources," but declined to give his authority.'

'Did he? I should like to have him in a witness box for five minutes. However, I can do without him. It was Dr. Bilde.'

'Then it 's true,' exclaimed Beryl Peyton, sadly ; he was thinking of Scarsdale's testimony, 'ask Mr. Ralph Dornay ; ask Dr. Bilde.'

But to Mr. Rennie, who was unaware of this, the remark seemed singularly inconsequent.

'I don't agree with your premisses, my dear Peyton,' he answered bluntly; but, as it happens, I do with your conclusions. Miss Marvon *has* a past of which she is ashamed.'

'Then there is no such thing as simplicity in women,' exclaimed the old man, sadly. 'And you, too, knew it and never told me.' He uttered a deep sigh and fell into his chair. 'It is my fate to be fooled by every one in whom I put trust.'

'It is the fate of most people, my dear Peyton,' answered the lawyer, quietly; 'but, as regards Miss Marvon, there is no cause, as far as I know, for disappointment. I said she was ashamed of her past, but not that she had reason for being ashamed of it. She has been weak, she *is* weak, but she is not guilty.'

'You would not say that if she was ten years older,' said the old man, gloomily. 'It is wonderful what extenuating circumstances even a lawyer will find in youth, if the culprit is a woman!'

Mr. Rennie opened his eyes to an extent that, upon his own account, they had rarely reached before.

'To make your cynic,' he murmured, 'there is certainly nothing like your thoroughgoing philanthropist soured. What I meant, Mr. Peyton,' he added aloud, 'was that Miss Marvon took a morbid view of her own position, which is simply that she has the misfortune to be of illegitimate birth.'

'Do you mean to say that 's all!' exclaimed the old man.

'I will lay my life on it,' said the lawyer. 'Dr. Bilde and the rest discovered something wrong and hoped for the worst, whereas they 've only found a mare's nest.'

'But it 's a positive advantage,' argued Beryl Peyton. 'No family ties—no leeches. Why, the girl is to be congratulated.'

'Well, I didn't do *that*,' said the lawyer, comically; 'but upon the circumstances coming to my knowledge, I did my best to combat her own morbid views upon the subject.'

'Poor thing, poor thing! And who were her parents?'

The lawyer played with his watchchain, and answered with an indifferent air, 'Well, the fact is, she doesn't know.'

'Good heavens! then they may be alive now, and when she has got a little money will be sure to turn up again. A woman who is well off is never in want of relatives.'

'They 're dead, both dead,' said Mr. Rennie, curtly.

'How can she know they 're dead if she doesn't know who they were?' was the quick reply.

'Somebody else knows—at least I suspect so. The matter is kept secret from her, probably for some good reason.'

'*I* must know!' ejaculated Mr. Peyton. His face had suddenly grown dark and frowning, and his lips trembled uneasily. They were saying to his inward ear, ' What did that woman mean by pitfalls ? '

' It is a secret that in my opinion ought to be respected,' argued Mr. Rennie.

' You know it then,' put in the old man, with a glance of keen suspicion.

' I do not know it, Mr. Peyton ; nor, since any allusion to it obviously gives the poor girl pain, have I sought to discover it. Why should you, of all men, who hold the ties of consanguinity so cheap, be solicitous to do so? Why should it not be sufficient for you to be assured—as I do now assure you—that Miss Marvon herself is without the shadow of reproach ? '

' No matter why : it is not sufficient. You have said that somebody else knows. You will be so good as to furnish me at once with that person's name.'

A flush came into the lawyer's face at the other's suspicious manner, but he answered drily enough, ' I thought I had already told you I only suspected who it was. I will go to that person, however, and if I have guessed right will endeavour to obtain the information you desire.'

'It is some one in this house, then?' exclaimed the other, vehemently, as the lawyer rose to leave the room.

'No, sir, it is not: it is some one out of the house.'

As the door closed upon his companion, Beryl Peyton drew a long breath of relief, and as he passed his hand across his forehead the furrows which angry suspicion had raised there slowly smoothed themselves away. If the some one who alone could solve this mystery was 'out of the house,' that person could not be his wife.

CHAPTER XLVIII.

' IT CAN BUT COST ME A CLIENT.'

THOUGH the lawyer had quitted Mr. Peyton's presence with an air of indifference, and as if bound on an errand of small importance, this was no indication of his real feelings: he had left his client, indeed, far more at ease than he was himself.

Though a man of few words, he gave attention to the words of others, and with his half-shut eyes saw more than any one suspected. During his stay at Letcombe Hall he had acquired, without eavesdropping, or chucking a lady's-maid under the chin, more information than Dr. Bilde and the two philosophers together. Unlike these gentlemen, however, he had learned quite enough, and was very unwilling to push his investigations further. But now it behoved him to push them. If Mr. Peyton had been content to take things as he found them, it would have been no part of Mr. Rennie's duty to stimulate his curiosity; but once his client had expressed a wish to know the truth, he had no alternative but, having found it, to communicate it to him. And he felt only too sure that whither his steps were now leading him—namely, to Bank Cottage— he was about to find it.

Mrs. Sotheran, as usual, was within doors: like most women of her nervous and apprehensive nature, she was a stay-at-home, content to let unfriendly Fate come to her own door rather than go forth to meet it. Even in her youth, when her step was elastic, and she drew her breath without being conscious of the process, exercise had had no charms for her. The fresh air is not for the feeble; the winds of heaven visit them too roughly and only serve to remind them of their weakness. And of late she had other reasons for remaining under her own roof. As the time drew near for her son's marriage with the girl whom she had learnt to love next to her son, a certain picture of a mediaeval type was always presenting itself to her morbid imagination—the figure of Beryl Peyton coming up the hill towards her cottage door with this inquiry coming scrollwise out of his mouth, 'Be so good as to tell me who is the young person calling herself Mary Marvon?'

That her son should be happily married and no questions asked seemed too much bliss to one who made such modest demands on fortune as the poor widow.

When she saw from her window Mr. Rennie leave the high-road and turn into the bridle path that led to her dwelling, she knew what he was come about as well as though he had already told her. She might almost have addressed him in the terms used by a lady of a similar temperament, who at last found a burglar under her bed, 'You are the very individual I have been looking for these twenty years.'

It is often the misfortune of this too-providential class to be miserable all their lives about a catastrophe that may never happen: on the other hand, they have certainly the advantage of being prepared for it.

It was with hands that did not tremble, though with a sinking heart, that she opened the door for her visitor, before he knocked at it, and ushered him into her neat little parlour: she was in expectation of the worst, and had strung her frail nature up to meet it.

'Why, one would really think you had expected my visit,' said the lawyer, cheerfully.

'I saw you coming up the hill!' she murmured evasively, and her head, which was still a pretty one, nodded spasmodically from side to side.

'What a pleasant house and a charming situation you have here!' said Mr. Rennie, who knew very well what that movement meant. 'For my part, I like this even better than the view from the Hall,' and he regarded the landscape through the window for a few moments as though he would like to buy it. ‘I just looked in for a word or two with you on a matter of business. Can you give me five minutes of your time, my dear Mrs. Sotheran, and alone?’

‘Susan is gone down the village, and Jane is in the kitchen,’ answered the widow; and with either of those young women she would very gladly have changed places for the remainder of her existence, if only the lawyer would not have said another word.

‘Very good, then, since we are liable to no interruption, I may say at once that the subject of our conversation will be Mary Marvon. You know all about her, of course.’

‘I know something; but what I know, Mr. Rennie, I am not at liberty to tell,’ said the widow. The words came glibly enough, for many a time she had rehearsed them in anticipation of some such an inquiry, but all her preparation could not keep her head from that nervous shaking, nor her frame from trembling in every limb.

'You are quite right to be reticent, Mrs. Sotheran : nothing is more natural than that you should say to yourself, " This is no business of Mr. Rennie's," nor, indeed, is it. I am here as the representative of Mr. Beryl Peyton, and at his express request. It is not unreasonable that he should wish to know something about the antecedents of this young lady, whom he is about to dower handsomely, and concerning whom I may confide to you he has also ulterior intentions. He wishes to be quite certain that these benefits will be conferred upon a person who is worthy of them.'

'I have known Mary Marvon from her birth,' said the widow, confidently, ' and have never seen aught but good in her. She is one in a thousand.'

'So far the Court is with you, Mrs. Sotheran,' said the lawyer, smiling : 'if you had said one in ten thousand—so far as I have any experience of young women—you might still plead justification. You say, however, you have known her from her birth: it is of her birth that I am here to make inquiry.'

'She is a suppositious child,' murmured the poor widow.

'A *what*, ma'am?'

'A suppositious—dear, dear, what am I saying! I mean a posthumous child.'

'Just so: her father died before she was born. Still, she must have had a father.'

There was a long pause: the widow stared at her companion as a bird awaiting deglutition stares at a snake, but uttered not a syllable.

'I suppose I should not be far wrong,' continued the lawyer blandly, 'if I called him Henry Peyton.'

'Gracious heavens, how did you know that?' exclaimed Mrs. Sotheran in a terrified whisper.

'I didn't know it till this minute, ma'am. I only guessed as much. She is illegitimate, of course.'

The widow nodded sideways, but she meant

assent. She was speechless with amazement at the other's sagacity.

'I am distressed to give you pain,' said the lawyer, kindly ; 'but, as I am sure you will understand, I have no choice. There is nothing to be alarmed at—that is, necessarily. It is a delicate case, but all will depend upon the treatment, and it will be in my hands. Only I must know the truth. Now, who was the mother ?'

Mrs. Sotheran's tongue seemed to cleave to her jaws : she opened her mouth twice as if for air, and then replied in the same hushed tones, ' Jane Lockwood.'

' That 's bad,' said the lawyer, mechanically. The words escaped him before he knew it, or he would have been careful not to add to his companion's apprehension by any dismal forecast of the future. ' That was the village organist, was it not—the girl he ran off with ?'

' Yes ; from Letcombe Hall.'

This local touch was full of significance : it was evident that, in the widow's eyes, it added to the crime of abduction, sacrilege.

' Mr. Peyton took it very much to heart, as I have heard.'

' He did, indeed : it separated him from his son altogether. It was a terrible time for all of us, and nearly broke Mrs. Peyton's heart. She never set eyes upon her Harry again.'

' Was Mr. Peyton as angry with the girl as with the young man, do you think ? ' inquired Mr. Rennie, thoughtfully.

' Not at first : at first he pitied her. But when his son refused to marry Miss Campbell of the Towers, which was the only condition upon which he would forgive him—you know the story, of course—he became furious against poor Jane, whose influence, he imagined, was still strong enough to prevent the match.'

' And was it so ? '

' Heaven knows. The report goes that he soon tired of her, and only refused to obey his father out of obstinacy.'

' But what do *you* think ? '

' I only saw the poor girl once, when Harry was in America. He may have deserted her (for she had not heard of him for many months), but she did not say so. Indeed she could scarcely have thought so, since she was so solicitous to obey his injunctions.'

'Now tell me, does Mrs. Peyton know of all this?'

'She does.'

Mr. Rennie's countenance fell.

'How could I help it?' pleaded the widow, pitifully. 'Would you have had me keep such a secret to myself? I am not made of stone or steel: and when she was pining away for her dead son, how could I forbear to tell her he had left a child behind him, her own flesh and blood?'

Mr. Rennie shook his head. What he meant to imply was that it was but a natural child, of which the law (which has but a bowing acquaintance with nature) could take no cognisance.

'Heaven knows,' continued Mrs. Sotheran, 'that I would have brought up the child as my own had that been possible; but how could I account for its possession, how bring it here, with a daily, nay hourly, lie on my lips? Instinct would have told the secret.'

' Then on learning the child's parentage,' pursued Mr. Rennie, ' Mrs. Peyton of course found the means for her support ? '

' She did. How could Mr. Peyton himself blame her for that? But she never saw the child, though she yearned to see her. She was content, rather than incur her husband's wrath, to ignore her; content that Mary should grow up an orphan waif, having no other friend than myself. Oh, sir, you are a man, and do not know a mother's heart, or you would pity her.'

' I do pity her,' returned the lawyer, gravely: ' if nothing had happened more than this, I could not blame her. But the girl is here, under her grandfather's roof, and without his knowledge.'

' I know. I know. Yes, that is terrible. But Mrs. Beckett—there was a quarrel between her and Mary—and the girl was suddenly cast adrift in London, nameless and friendless : no, not friendless, Mr. Rennie, for she has told me how good a friend you yourself have been to her. You will not desert her now. Oh, promise me you will not desert her now.'

'I am not thinking of *her*,' said the lawyer, gravely. 'She has friends enough—means enough, and an honest man to love her. I am thinking of Mrs. Peyton.'

'And I too, Mr. Rennie. Do not think I have forgotten her even for a moment. Her husband will never forgive her—never, never. It will kill her.'

'Let us hope it will not be so bad as that. But how could she have done anything so rash, knowing what he is, as to bring the girl here—under his very roof?'

'I have thought of that; nay, I have thought of nothing else from the first hour she came. But having seen her—that was the fatal step—having once seen her, she could not resist it.'

'The lawyer stroked his chin. He knew

that Mrs. Peyton had made up her mind to receive Mary as her companion before her interview with her at Mr. Tidman's establishment; but being a man, he felt it was not worth while to hark back on that. It is only women who cry over spilt milk.

'It is certain that Mr. Peyton is very fond of the girl,' he observed meaningly.

'How could he help it?' observed the widow, naïvely.

'And you are sure Mary knows nothing of her parentage—guesses nothing, and is therefore absolutely ignorant of the deception—for such he will consider it—that has been practised upon him?'

'Nothing, nothing.'

'Then I will bring them together,' exclaimed the lawyer, vehemently, 'and tell the whole story before them both.'

'Oh, indeed you must not do that. You do not know Mary Marvon, or how she holds her mother's memory: *that* is sacred to her, but for her father's unknown relatives she feels only loathing and contempt. Directly she found out in what relation they stood to her, she refused to take another farthing from them. That was another reason why Mrs. Peyton was compelled to give her a home at Letcombe Dottrell. She was bent on earning her own living rather than receive their alms.'

'I remember,' said Mr. Rennie, thinking of the type-writer and his copyist. 'Mary is a very resolute young woman.'

'Resolute! You don't know Mary Marvon. She will tell Mr. Peyton to his face that his son was a scoundrel.'

'Quite right,' said Mr. Rennie, rubbing his hands. 'I think I see my way. She couldn't do better. It will only be a corroboration of his own view.'

'But she will spare nobody, not even Mr. Peyton himself. She will tell him, "Your wife has done all she could—because all she dared —to repair the sin of her son; but *you*—you have done nothing."'

'But how could he, when he *knew* nothing?'

said Mr. Rennie, smiling. 'A young lady may be resolute, surely, without being unreasonable. At all events, I'll try it.' 'At the worst,' muttered the lawyer to himself, 'it can but cost me a client.'

CHAPTER XLIX.

A DISCOVERY.

Mr. Rennie had his hand on the door when he suddenly recollected something.

'By-the-by, you used a phrase a few minutes ago, Mrs. Sotheran, which I should like to have explained. It may be of no consequence, but in a matter of this kind one should not leave a stone unturned. You said, and the remark showed your knowledge of human nature, that Jane Lockwood could hardly have imagined herself deserted by Henry Peyton, or she would not have been so solicitous to obey his injunctions. Now what were those injunctions?'

'I—they—I cannot tell you,' gasped the widow: 'I have told enough.'

'Pardon me, my dear madam, but you, whose feelings are so manifestly interested in the matter, can hardly be the best judge of that.'

'She was on her deathbed when she spoke to me, Mr. Rennie. If you had but seen her, and heard how solemnly she addressed me, in the presence only of her unconscious child!'

'I wish I had,' said the lawyer, gently; 'for then it would have been unnecessary to have put you to this pain. It is, remember, for the child's sake that I plead.'

'Would you have me break my promise to the dead?' exclaimed the widow, clasping her trembling hands. 'She may be looking on us even now!'

The lawyer crossed his legs and put his finger-tips together—his attitude when instructing counsel.

'My dear Mrs. Sotheran, this matter has been fully argued, fought out, and settled. It is the case of the pious founder. He was generally anything but pious; a scoundrel who, having lived disreputably, sought, by a posthumous liberality which cost him nothing, to atone for his past misdeeds. But let us take the strongest case, and suppose him pious. Upon his deathbed (a very bad place, by the way, to arrange plans for the benefit of posterity) he made certain arrangements for the public good. Twenty years afterwards (as in the present case), or two hundred years—it doesn't matter—the circumstances under which he made these plans entirely alter: what he intended to be a benefit becomes a nuisance to everybody, and the law very properly steps in and makes them of no effect. No doubt Jane Lockwood meant to do her best for her little daughter, but how could she know that the girl would be one day under Beryl Peyton's roof, and engaged to be married to your son? You say that she may be looking on us even now. She possibly may: that is a question which not even the Court of Chancery has the power to settle. But even supposing she is a spectator, she is not a Witness of whom we can make much. She is unable to inform us of her present wishes. We may take it for granted, however, that they are in favour of her child—that she desires us to do all we can to insure her happiness. If what she said to you has no tendency to do so, there will be no harm done : what you tell me will then go in at one ear and out at the other. I have too much to do to interest myself, unless in the way of business, in the affairs of any young woman alive or dead. If, on the other hand, what you have to say is of importance to Mary Marvon, you may do her a very grievous wrong by concealing it.'

It was Mr. Rennie's way to take a practical and commonplace view of most things—in which he now and then made a great mistake— but, as it happened, he could not under the circumstances have adopted a more judicious line with his present companion. His coolness, his confidence, and his total want of sympathy with the morbid excitement under which she laboured, tended to steady her nerves.

' After all,' she answered, ' what poor Jane Lockwood said to me was very little. But she left behind her a sacred charge. It was a desk, given her no doubt by the man who wronged her, while she still believed in him, and in her eyes of priceless value.'

' Nevertheless it was not, I conclude, an empty desk,' observed the lawyer, drily.

' I don't know—that is, of course, I never opened it, Mr. Rennie,' pleaded the widow, vehemently, like one who is making his last stand against overwhelming odds. ' I not only gave my word to that dying woman, but took heaven to witness that that desk should never be given up, save to Henry Peyton.'

' A dead man at the time you made the promise, madam.'

' No matter: I cannot commit perjury.'

' Still, unless you burn the desk and its contents, which would be a very strong measure, when you are dead and gone some one will open it.'

' After my death you shall burn it,' said

Mrs. Sotheran, with the air of one who bestows a favour.

'You are very good, but that is a treat which must needs be reserved for your executor. Is it possible, my dear madam, you do not perceive that Jane Lockwood laid this injunction upon you under the impression that her lover was alive, but that being dead you are placed in the position of his representative? In not opening that desk, Mrs. Sotheran, you have neglected a sacred duty for the last twenty years.'

'Heaven forgive me!' ejaculated the poor lady, 'I never thought of that'—and she burst into tears.

'It is a sin of omission, my dear madam,' said the lawyer, soothingly, 'which, considering the amount of active misdoing we commit, is not worth crying about. It is as it were but a portion of that peck of dirt which we are all said to eat in our lives without knowing it. Such an error would be serious, however, if, being convinced of it, we did not make haste to repair it. I conclude you have got the key as well as the desk.'

'I have worn it round my neck for twenty years,' replied the poor lady.

'Dear me, that is being a trustee with a vengeance,' exclaimed the lawyer, admiringly. 'I should clank like a ghost if I took such care of my clients' property as all that. The desk I suppose you hardly—ah, in the sitting-room upstairs, is it? I will not trouble you to fetch it : we will go together.'

After such work to catch his fish, the lawyer was much too wise to let it out of his sight. He had seen too many, apparently well landed on the bank, disappear with a flap of their tails into the river. From a cupboard in the little drawing-room in which no one could think of looking for anything of importance, Mrs. Sotheran produced the desk, and gave the key to her companion.

'I have your permission, I conclude, to open it,' said Mr. Rennie, with professional caution.

'I have nothing to say to it, one way or the other,' replied the poor lady, wringing her hands. Her superstitious fears, aroused by the sight of the desk, seemed to have once more gained possession of her. 'The matter is now in your hands, and I will have nothing to do with it.'

'Very good,' returned the lawyer, not displeased with an arrangement which gave him liberty of action, untrammelled by illogical scruples. 'Henceforth I will take the whole responsibility of it, and reserve to myself the right of communicating to you my discoveries, or withholding them.'

In the desk there was but one piece of folded paper, which the lawyer opened, glanced at, and then quietly placed in his pocket-book.

Mrs. Sotheran watched him with half-averted eyes, as nervous folks look at a precipice. But when he began, 'It 's only a memorandum, which may or may not be of importance,' she thrust her fingers into her ears.

‘ I don't want to hear anything about it at all,’ she exclaimed with vehemence.

‘ All right, madam, you shan't,’ bawled the lawyer. Then, dropping his voice, he added, ‘ You are sure that it was in respect to that slip of paper that Jane Lockwood enjoined secrecy ? ’

‘ I am quite sure.’

‘ She gave you the idea, I suppose, of a very self-sacrificing woman,’ said Mr. Rennie, thoughtfully.

‘ Yes, indeed : she loved not wisely but too well. She always seemed to me the gentlest of created beings, and even to the last had not one word to say against the man that wronged her.’

‘ That was so, was it ? ’ said the lawyer, thoughtfully.

‘ And what are you going to do about it all, Mr. Rennie ? ’ inquired the widow, anxiously, as her companion rose from his chair. ‘ How grave you look ! Surely things are no worse than they were five minutes ago.’

'I don't know; I can't tell,' said the other, evasively. 'Let it suffice you to learn that what I have found is of great importance and ought to be known; and that to have concealed it would have been to wrong the dead and the living.'

'Thank heaven for that, and you for your good advice,' exclaimed the widow, fervently. 'I feel as if a mountain had been removed from me.'

As Mr. Rennie moved down the hill towards the Hall, you would have said that the mountain had been shifted to his own shoulders. His steps were slow, his brow was heavy with thought, and his lips moved uneasily. 'If the man were like anybody else,' they murmured, 'we should have victory all along the line. But as it is, no one can tell how he 'll take it.'

CHAPTER L.

AN EXPLOSION.

THE party were all at luncheon when Mr. Rennie reached the Hall; and, as he was far too wise a man to suffer the cares of business to interfere with the pleasures of appetite, he joined them. As he took his usual seat by Mr. Peyton's side, the latter flashed an inquiring glance at him which also—such is the perfection of the human heliograph—included Mary Marvon. '*Sans peur et sans reproche,*' whispered the lawyer. 'I would have laid my life on it,' answered the old man, and his eye rested on the unconscious lovers at the other end of the table with a well-satisfied look. He had had so many disappointments in his *protégés,* that a little triumph where his good opinion had been justified was excusable. He regarded his wife also with an unusual tenderness, born of the consciousness that he had gone near to wrong her in his thoughts; so sensitive, so sympathetic is the philanthropist at large, when the bark of his benevolence has a fair wind with her, and there are no chopping seas to obstruct her course. Never had the host's manner been more genial, never had his smile 'warmed the cockles of the heart' of every member of the Happy Family, save two, more than upon this occasion. It was true that his eye avoided those of the two philosophers, who shuddered like Lascars in the snow in consequence; but, when they were not looking at him, it regarded them with a glance that was by no means devoid of humour. When the meal was at an end, he beckoned the butler: 'Barkham,' he said, 'bring me a Bradshaw.' Then, after consulting it carefully through his gold spectacles, he observed with great distinctness—

'Mr. Marks and Mr. Nayler, your train, I

perceive, starts at half past four. A carriage
will be at the door for you at 3.20 precisely.'

The nature of this intimation, so delicately
conveyed, was understood only by those to
whom it was addressed. To them, if it had
been an imperial ukase, dated from St. Peters-
burg, it could not have signified more plainly
that they were banished to Siberia—the Siberia
of personal expenses and landladies with lodg-
ing accounts. They knew they were expelled
from Eden, and had incurred the curse of
Labour: that they were about to exchange a
land flowing with milk and honey for a barren
soil. You may tickle the public with philosophy
for many a year before it laughs with a harvest.

The offenders, however, took their punishment with great dignity. One might have said
(if one had not known them) that nothing
became their life at Letcombe Hall so much as
their manner of leaving it. They only bowed
and smiled, as though their carriage had been
bespoken for them for an excursion of pleasure,
just as a Japanese noble, on receiving the im-

perial commands to make himself scarce, proceeds cheerfully to disembowel himself with one of the two swords he always carries about with him. It was not, however, their respective systems of philosophy which enabled them thus gallantly to meet the hour of trial. They had beheld other members of the Happy Family banished from their patron's presence—and come back again like the sun in April. His favour was capricious, and they by no means gave up hope of once more basking in his smile. I am sorry to say that their gentle confederate, Scarsdale, who had received a similar intimation through the mouth of the valet, received her sentence with less resignation. Perhaps she took shorter views, and was of a less sanguine temperament, but the manner in which she 'went on' in the servants' hall, and in the presence of the gentleman she had understood (but this, it now appeared, was a mistake) had been betrothed to her, was quite appalling.

Mr. Ralph Dornay's man, who had seen

something of town life, afterwards described the scene to his master as reminding him of what happens in a police court when some too excitable lady, on receiving sentence, takes off her shoe, and, with a few appropriate words, hurls it at the administrator of justice. It would have been impossible to imagine, had she not mentioned him very pointedly by name, that Miss Scarsdale's language could have been applied to a person of such respectability and position as Mr. Beryl Peyton. She was extradited in a vehicle by herself, to the great relief of her fellow-culprits, in whom the apprehensions of her company had, not without reason, greatly increased the terrors of exile.

At the conclusion of the midday meal, Mr. Rennie accompanied Mr. Peyton to his sanctum. The lawyer wore a cheerful countenance, but beneath it there lay as much solicitude as a man of business can afford to feel in the affairs of others. His client, on the other hand, was in high spirits.

'So there was no great mystery about

the young lady, after all?' were his first words.

'I didn't say there was no mystery, Mr. Peyton. I only implied, as we both expected, that there was nothing to be ashamed of.'

'There *is* a secret then, is there? Well, I'll answer for it you have ferreted it out.'

'I have,' answered the lawyer, gravely. 'The question is, however, since Miss Marvon is ignorant of her parentage, whether more people than necessary should know it. Will it not suffice you, Mr. Peyton, to have my word for it, that your proposed bounty will not be ill-disposed? Why seek to look into a matter past and gone, the revelation of which can only give pain to an innocent girl?'

'If you can give me the assurance that the matter does not concern me,' replied the old man—then, suddenly breaking off with a fierce, imperious look, he added sharply, 'But I know it *does* concern me. What is it?'

'That it has some "connection" with you,

Mr. Peyton, I cannot deny ; though when I call to mind your views, so often expressed upon a certain subject, I can hardly say "concern."'

Mr. Peyton started to his feet as though he had been five-and-twenty, and in a voice shrill with hate and rage exclaimed, 'She is that fellow's daughter who called himself my son !'

'She *is* your son's daughter,' answered the lawyer, quietly ; 'but remember, she does not know it.'

'That is a lie!' exclaimed the old man, passionately : 'she is a treacherous, lying girl. It is a conspiracy. Who is her confederate ? Do you hear me ?'

'It seems to me, Mr. Peyton,' said the lawyer, meeting the other's furious look full face, 'that you have not heard *me*. Since the girl is unaware of the circumstances of her birth, how can she have a confederate ? If, however, you wish to know who was my informant in this matter, it was Mrs. Sotheran.'

'Ay, I thought so,' cried the old man,

striking his hand upon the table. 'She sent for her son here to marry *my* son's bastard.'

'Permit me to observe that you sent for him yourself,' observed Mr. Rennie, drily. 'I have your letter in which you say as much. You even write in it that his coming will be a pleasant surprise for Mrs. Sotheran. How, therefore, could she have foreseen what was to happen here?'

'It never will happen,' said Beryl Peyton, grimly. Then, after a long pause, 'Who was her mother?'

'Jane Lockwood.'

Beryl Peyton uttered a frightful imprecation. 'So her brat has been palmed off upon me, has she, to be the prop of my old age and the comfort of my declining years! A little too soon, however, as she shall find. Yes, I see it all now: the woman Sotheran was always hand in glove with the girl till she disgraced herself and fled from this roof. She was sent for when the girl died, and brought back a lying tale of the child being dead too. It is a plot that has been twenty years maturing, and promised a fair harvest, but the crop has failed. As for her accomplice, Miss Marvon——'

'She is no accomplice,' said Mr. Rennie, firmly.

' Tool or accomplice, it is all one,' cried the old man, vehemently. ' So help me Heaven, I will never see her baseborn face again.'

It needed Heaven, it seemed, or some power beyond his own, to help him in this resolve, for his face worked and his eyes softened as he uttered it. 'If the fraud had lasted longer,' he continued bitterly, ' I should have wasted more than what she sought upon her, for I had almost learnt to love her.'

' As to seeing Miss Marvon's face again,' said Mr. Rennie, gravely, ' you may do that and yet not break your oath, for she is not baseborn.'

' What ? '

' Listen, and then be deaf to the voice of nature if you please. When Jane Lockwood lay a-dying, with her child beside her in its cradle, she did the noblest thing that ever woman did. Your son had left her, and had long been dead, but she thought him living. He had laid his commands upon her to keep a certain document—I have it here—secret from every eye except his own. She knew what it was, and that the production of it would clear her fair name from stain. Yet sooner than disobey him, and by this disclosure destroy, perhaps, the last hope of reconciliation with yourself, she died, in Mrs. Sotheran's presence, patiently enduring her pity, if not contempt, and consenting to be thought to be your son's mistress, when she was his lawful wife. This is the certificate of his marriage.'

A wolfish light came into the old man's eyes as he murmured ' Give it me.'

' No, I will not give it to you, Mr. Peyton, till I learn what you intend to do with it.'

' To tear it—to burn it ! ' cried the other, in a voice half choked with passion. ' Bid the girl leave this house at once: not a moment longer shall it shelter one of that serpent's brood.'

'She is your son's lawful daughter, sir; your own grandchild,' said the lawyer, quietly.

'I believe it; that is why I hate her,' shrieked the old man. 'Frail as her mother, false as her father, bid her go, I tell you, or I will push her forth with my own hands;' and as he spoke he made a stride towards the door.

'Stay, sir, stay,' exclaimed the lawyer, with dignity. 'If you are indeed resolved upon this most unnatural and unjust proceeding, let it at least be put into effect with decency.'

'Do as you will, but bid her begone, spawn of an ingrate, her and her lover too, and may my curse go with them.' The vehemence and rage of the old man's tone were terrible, but not worse than the expression of his face, which seemed to blaze with hate and fury. The lawyer regarded him with a steadfast look.

'If I thought you were master of yourself, Mr. Peyton,' he said, 'I would say to you a word or two of truth, though they should be

the last I ever spoke to you. But as it is I
will but do your bidding: not that it is my
office, nor that of any man who respects himself, to carry out such infamous injunctions, but
because in my mouth they will be less offensive
to those who must needs obey them than in
yours.'

CHAPTER LI.

LAWYER AND CLIENT.

MR. RENNIE, who knew his client and his ungovernable passions well, felt that there was no time to be lost in performing his unpleasant mission to the young people. It was a wet day, and it was their custom of an afternoon, as he remembered, to pass their time in such weather in the library. Mary was fond of reading, and whatever volume chanced to be engaging her attention had a marvellous attraction for Charley. A duplicate would not serve his turn. She complained—though not bitterly—that she could never get a book to herself, nor even look at an illustration without his shadow crossing it.

One lesson from one book they read.

They were reading it when the lawyer entered—that is to say, Mary was reading it, and Charley, sitting on the arm of her chair, was reading Mary ; studying her downcast eyes, and would-be serious mouth, and steadying himself for the task (for how can a young man use application unless he is steady?) with his hand upon her shoulder—' a sight to make an old man young.'

' Mary,' said the lawyer, gravely, ' I have bad news for you—bad news for you both.'

' Good heavens, what has happened? ' exclaimed Charley.

' A great deal ; far more than I can tell you in the time at my disposal. Mr. Peyton has just discovered that his son contracted marriage with the young lady with whom, as you have doubtless heard, he fled from this very roof some twenty years ago.'

' How can that be bad news? ' inquired Charley. ' Mr. Peyton must surely be glad to find that his unhappy son was not so black as he has been painted.'

The lawyer shook his head. 'In marrying Jane Lockwood he filled, in his father's eyes, the cup of his filial disobedience ; in the keeping that marriage secret he has crowned a life of duplicity and deceit. Such, at least, is the view which I conclude Mr. Peyton has taken of it, for he is almost out of his mind with hate and rage.'

' But are they not both dead?' murmured Mary, in a horrified whisper. ' In such a case one forgives even a murderer.'

' Yes, my dear girl, they are dead ; but I know by sad experience that, where kin hates kin, the tomb itself is no asylum. I am bound to say,' continued the lawyer, not forgetful even in that moment of keenest exasperation that the offender was his client, ' that if Henry Peyton could have had his will, he would have doomed his father to a more dreadful fate than death.'

' And was he as bad a husband as a son?' inquired Mary, with a half-incredulous glance at her lover's face, as if in the vain attempt to picture him with a fault or two.

'I cannot tell. He had a wife, I know, whose self-sacrifice would have made her worthy of the best of husbands—a loving, patient woman, in whom duty survived death itself.'

'And could not her love plead for her husband with his father ?' said Mary, softly.

'No ; when nature fails in us, my dear young lady, good itself works for evil. It was that very love which he could forgive in her least of all.'

'And yet Mr. Peyton has been so good to us,' sighed Mary. 'It seems impossible to believe such things of him. Oh, Mr. Rennie, can all this be true ? '

'It is quite true, and there is more and worse behind,' answered the lawyer, gravely. 'Mr. Peyton has heard for the first time to-day that this unhappy pair left offspring— an orphan daughter still survives them.'

'Thank heaven!' exclaimed Mary, fervently: 'in her he can retrieve the past.'

'Quite right,' said Charley, cheerfully. 'I see what your bad news amounts to now. The heir is found; the Happy Family breaks up like the Round Table, and all have once more to seek their fortunes. I have found mine,' he added gently, stooping to kiss Mary's forehead; 'and if we have to wait a little longer for our happiness, and, when it does come, to live upon bread and cheese instead of kickshaws provided by a rich man's bounty, ·what matters? I thank him all the same, since it was through him I won her; nor do I grudge this new-found Miss Kilmansegg her acres or her guineas.'

The lawyer glanced at the young man approvingly. 'If I had a daughter of my own,' he thought, 'this is the sort of young fellow— if he could only make a decent settlement— that I should choose for a son-in-law.' 'No, my good lad,' he said, 'this orphan will prove no heiress, and robs you in another way. Her grandfather has closed his heart against her, and spurns her from his roof. Mary Peyton, for such indeed you are, my dear young lady,' and the lawyer laid his hand upon her head with great solemnity, 'I am here, though very unwillingly, to bid you leave it.'

'It's a strange story!' exclaimed Charley, in amazement, not unmixed with some incredulity, for in his experience in the Probate Office he had known mistakes to be made even by lawyers; but Mary, who knew Mr. Rennie better, burst into tears.

'There is nothing to regret, my dear,' said the latter, gently. 'Remember how long it is since both your parents left all trouble and sorrow behind them.'

To this word of comfort, which doubtless owed its suggestion to the statute of limitations, Mary replied by a grateful look; but what she was thanking him for in her heart of hearts was the way in which he had spoken of her mother. How reverently too had Mrs. Sotheran always done so; but not, she remembered with a pang, not Mrs. Peyton. Of the memory of her son, indeed, that lady had shown herself mindful enough, but of the girl whom, as she believed, that son had betrayed, she had spoken nothing. She had good reasons, as we know, for never mentioning Jane Lockwood's name, but poor Mary did not know them. She naturally imagined that she ignored her. Mrs. Peyton had endeared herself to the girl in a thousand ways, and Mary loved her; but at this moment, when she seemed to have just found her mother, she felt averse from all who had turned a cold shoulder on her.

'I am ready to leave this house at once,' she answered calmly. 'Mrs. Sotheran, I know, will take me in.'

'Quite right—a capital plan,' exclaimed the lawyer: 'take her up to your mother's house, Charley, where she can await events. There is no knowing how things may turn out here in a day or two, though they look uncommonly black at present. Let her put on her bonnet and be off at once, lad,' he added earnestly, as

Mary, with a whispered word to her lover, was about to leave the room. ' If her grandfather sets eyes on her there will be a scene that they may both repent, for the girl does not want for spirit.'

' She wishes, however, to see her grand-mother before she goes,' said Charley : ' it is but for a kiss of farewell.'

' A dangerous thing at all times,' returned the lawyer, grimly, ' but in this case mid-summer madness. Such an interview is not to be thought of. If Beryl Peyton, whose head is already full of jealousy and mistrust, should find her speaking with his wife, he would sus-pect some new conspiracy. Be off, be off with you both.'

After having seen the young people safely upon their way, with a facetious promise, in-tended to sustain their spirits, that their per-sonal luggage should be respected and sent after them, even if he should find himself unable to protect their interests, the lawyer returned to his client, whose state of mind he had by no means exaggerated. The half-hour of solitude which Mr. Peyton had passed during the other's absence, so far indeed from having allayed his excitement, seemed to have increased it.

'Is she gone?' he exclaimed with vehemence. 'Has the seed of that viper left the house?'

'If you mean your granddaughter,' said the lawyer, drily, 'that young lady has gone to Bank Cottage.' He purposely stated the place where she had taken refuge, lest the knowledge that she had quitted Letcombe Dottrell should tend to familiarise the sense of estrangement, and thereby make any act of harshness that he might have in his mind more easy for him. In the tumult of his hate and passions, however, this hint escaped the old man's notice. 'And her lover?' he continued in a shrill, chill tone—'the boy that under the guise of frankness has been plotting to feather his nest both for him and her—has the boy gone too?'

'Charles Sotheran is also no longer a burthen on your hospitality, sir.'

'So far so good. Not a moment shall be lost in making sure that neither of them shall reap any benefit from me in any other manner. Bring me my will.'

'Which will?' inquired the lawyer, grimly; 'there are half a dozen of them, none of which, for some inscrutable reason, you have allowed me to destroy.'

'I have kept them, Mr. Rennie, as mementoes of the baseness of mankind, and as guide-stones, such as the coastguard use upon our downs by night, to warn me against the depths of duplicity and ingratitude.'

'Let us hope they will keep you on the straight road of common-sense for the future,' was the lawyer's quiet reply.

'Bring me my will, I say; the will I signed the other day, before I knew my confidence was being abused, by which I made provision for these harpies. As they have forfeited my bounty while I live, so shall they fail to inherit one farthing of my wealth when I am dead and gone.'

'Then may I ask, Mr. Peyton, who is to inherit it?'

'The man to whom the half of it is already bequeathed—Edgar Dornay.'

'And is it your serious purpose to make that young man, whom you have known but a few weeks, and only as a casual guest, your heir?'

'Why not?' exclaimed the old man, passionately. 'He is neither kith nor kin of mine. There is no tie of blood—no blood-poison—between him and me. Why not? I have not known him long, 'tis true; it is my experience that the more one knows of men, the more one regrets the knowledge. Yes, Edgar Dornay shall be my heir; and since he has certain highflying notions, such as I had myself before I knew the world, and of what stuff my fellow-men were made. which may induce him to share my bounty with certain unworthy persons, I will thank you to so contrive it as to put such misplaced generosity out of his power.'

'I will draw up no such will,' said Mr. Rennie, firmly.

'You will not! How dare you say so?' cried the old man, imperiously. 'Can I not leave my wealth to whom I like?'

'Rather say, Mr. Peyton, to keep from those you hate: nay—for you have not even the excuse of personal antagonism—to keep from the innocent offspring of one you hate.'

'My money is my own,' answered the old man, coldly.

'No doubt: yet hear me, Beryl Peyton. Whatever your faults, you have never been ungenerous or ungrateful; and since just now it is vain to expect you to listen to reason, I appeal to you to hold your hand in this miserable business, as a friend to whom you owe something, and for one thing, your present liberty; the power not only to perform what you have in your mind, but the simplest actions —to breathe the free air of heaven, for example. But for me you would be now in a madhouse.'

'I know it,' answered the old man, sternly. 'And who would have placed me there? My own, my only son. If there had been a chance of my being moved to weakness in this matter, if some fond memory of that viper, when in his childhood, and before he had begun to waste his life, had stirred within me, and pleaded for his child, that hint of yours would have crushed it. I thank you for the reminder, Mr. Rennie. You have been my friend. I acknowledge it fully; if I have not given you material proofs of the gratitude I owe you, that is not my fault; you could have had them if you pleased, and you can have them still. But please to remember that while you are my friend, you are also my lawyer.'

'I say again, Mr. Peyton, that I will draw up no such will.'

'Then you have lost a client. This very hour I will send to Lorton for Macalister, and he shall have my instructions.'

'Do so,' exclaimed the lawyer, laying his hand upon the door, and flashing upon the other a parting glance of hostility and contempt. 'Do so, and when that will is drawn, and you are dead, and powerless to commit more injustice, I 'll drive a coach and four through it.'

CHAPTER LII.

SEVERED.

AT Bank Cottage the exiled pair were welcomed with fear and trembling. With pale and terrified face the widow listened to her son's explanation of what had taken place at the Hall, and, even while clasping Mary to her breast. regretted her presence.

Her first words when he had finished were, ' And what of Mrs. Peyton?'

' Mary wished to see her,' said Charley, ' but Mr. Rennie would not hear of it. He said that if Mr. Peyton found them together, even though taking farewell, he would suspect they were in league against him.'

' And so he would,' murmured the widow. ' Has not Mr. Peyton seen her since all this happened?'

'Seen Mary?'

'No, no; his wife. Hark! what is that?' There was a sound of galloping hoofs in the lane beneath, and Mr. Flay flashed by on his pony at full speed. The kindly little doctor did not so much as raise his hat as he passed by them : he looked like one who rides for life and death.

'There must be something the matter at the Hall,' said Charley, apprehensively.

'God help poor Hilda!' muttered the widow, devoutly. That she called Mrs. Peyton by her Christian name was itself significant of her fears.

'If anything has happened to—to grand-mamma,' said Mary, earnestly, 'I *must* go to her.'

'Not for worlds!' exclaimed Mrs. Sotheran. 'You can do no good, my darling, and may do a world of harm.'

'But she has been so good and dear to me,' sobbed Mary, breaking down for the first time; 'and am I not her own flesh and blood?'

'That is a plea that will serve you little, my darling—save with her own sweet self. If, as I fear, your grandfather's wrath is roused against her, the sight of you would only add fuel to its flame. I knew it would one day come to this,' murmured the widow to herself. 'How could you—could you be so rash, Hilda?'

The three stood at the open window in silence, looking down the beautiful valley, steeped in the calm of evening and the freshness of the spring. But their eyes were fixed only on that spot where the towers of the Hall were visible. The air was full of quiet country sounds, but their ears listened only to some hoof-tread or footfall which should herald a messenger from the great house.

Nevertheless, to one of them, for years to come, that landscape, with its pleasant fields and farms, was to recur again and again in every detail of sight and sound—the cow that stood by the gap and chewed the cud; the milkmaid, as unconscious of domestic catastrophe as her patient charge; nay, the very creak of the unseen cartwheel in the road.

After a weary hour of suspense and strained attention, the news came. The doctor's pony once more appeared over the brow of the hill. As it drew slowly near, as though there was no need for its rider to hurry now, he made with head and hand a melancholy gesture. All seemed to know the burthen of his tale before he told it, and listened with bowed head. 'It is the last chapter of the old story,' said Mr. Flay, addressing the widow: 'I always told you how it would end.'

Mrs. Sotheran hid her face and burst into tears. Not so did Mary.

'There must have been some cause,' she said, putting aside Charley's encircling arm as though it was no time for softness, and speaking with earnest gravity; 'even women do not die of nothing.'

'Poor Mrs. Peyton died of heart complaint, from which she had suffered for years,' replied

the doctor, looking curiously at his inter-
locutor; 'there was some shock, no doubt.'

'Was my—was her husband with her when
she died?' inquired Mary.

'Not at the moment—no; just before, as I
understand.'

'I thought so.' The accusation and conviction in her tone were terrible.

'Mary, Mary! say no more,' whispered
Charley, imploringly. 'What good can come
of saying, even if it be so?'

His argument, it is probable, prevailed less
with her than the sense of obedience one day
to be owed to him; but she held her peace.
Of the fact, however—which was only too true
—she felt persuaded, namely, that Beryl Peyton's
anger had killed his wife. He had spoken
daggers, but used none.

It would have been a satisfaction to the
believers in heredity, because a corroboration
of their theory, to see the set determined look
that took the place of Mary Peyton's smile as
she uttered those three words, 'I thought so.'

What she was saying to herself was what she afterwards repeated to Lady Orr, who called at Bank Cottage, full of sympathy for Mary, immediately after the catastrophe, and on the eve of her immediate departure from the Hall, ' Well for him that he has disowned me, for never will I own him for kin of mine ! '

Then, with all the woman once more in her face, she turned to the weeping widow, and, mingling her tears with hers, sobbed out, ' *You are my mother now*; the only one near and dear to me in all the world ! '

' Save Charley, my own darling,' answered Mrs. Sotheran, soothingly.

' There is no need to remind her of that, mother,' said Charley, gently, ' for Mary and I are one.'

What Charley thus stated, somewhat in advance of the fact, was less so than he imagined, for it is certain that in that hour of sorrow it never struck him that Mrs. Peyton's death, by giving him the means to marry upon, would accelerate his own happiness.

For many a day, however, sorrow made her abode with the little household at Bank Cottage. It was dreadful to Mary, and hardly less so to Mrs. Sotheran, to feel that Mrs. Peyton lay unburied so near them, and they forbidden to press one kiss of farewell on the cold lips that had so often breathed their names. Even the cross of white flowers they wrought for her coffin lid was returned to them by Mr. Peyton's orders.

From their windows only did they venture to behold that long procession (albeit it comprised no such true mourners as themselves) wind along the road beneath them to the village churchyard; but Mr. Rennie, who, himself unbidden, found place among the crowd, told them all that passed. Though Beryl Peyton stood alone and watched with tearless eyes the vault shut in the dead—the faithful woman who loved him to the last, and who would have loved him more could he have hated others less—it was the lawyer's conviction that the nerve which sustained the man was strained to the utter-

most. 'His will is iron,' he said, 'but his heart
is wax. His hand will never clasp mine again;
it is his own harsh error that has sundered us.
But this I will say for him, that no man has
taken more delight in making others happy,
has done more good without a thought of self,
has striven more to make the rough places
smooth for tender feet, than Beryl Peyton.
Wealth and power have been his ruin; they
have made him draw too proud a breath. In
the plenitude of his greatness and in the certi-
tude of his own good intentions, he has forgotten that, however well one may play the
part of Providence to the unthankful and the
evil, it is God alone to whom vengeance be-
longeth. He feels it now, though he will
never confess it; and that conviction—I read
it in his face as it turned towards home to-day
—will be his deathblow.'

The lawyer's judgment, even when it had
no connection with his calling, was seldom at
fault, and soon after Mrs. Peyton's funeral Mr.
Flay began to make professional visits to the

Hall with unwonted frequency. Charley had long returned to town and his office duties, and concerning her grandfather, whether for good or ill, Mary's mouth was sealed. But the widow, who, now that the worst had happened, had lost her nervous fears of the master of the Hall, was very curious to know how things were going on there. The doctor's report of his patient, though given with professional caution, was gloomy enough. He described him as passing entire days without speaking, save by signs to the deaf mute, and, at the best, as being very silent and apathetic. He still, however, took the head of his table, and matters went on much as usual, except that many things which he had formerly looked after in person were now superintended by Mr. Edgar Dornay. It was understood on all sides that, in case of anything happening to the Squire, that young gentleman would be his heir; but in the meantime the Happy Family were entertained as usual. The two philosophers, forgiven doubtless because they had plotted against

the object of their patron's enmity, had had
their sentence remitted after a few days of
banishment, and were again in clover; but
Miss Scarsdale, less wise in her generation, and
who knew not how to be patient under punishment, was in exile presumably for life.

' And what will become of them all, do you
think, Mr. Flay, when Mr. Beryl Peyton goes?'
inquired Mrs. Sotheran.

' Oh, after him the Deluge,' said the little
doctor, who had no love for those parasites,
especially for the philosophic ones. ' When
the sewers are flushed it is impossible, you
know, to tell where the rats go.'

Thus life ran its smooth round at Bank
Cottage till midsummer came round, with its
month of vacation (for a holiday granted to a
great man's *protégé* counts for nothing) for
Charley.

' I hope, my dear,' said Mrs. Sotheran one
day to Mary, with a little more simplicity, I 'm
afraid, than naturally belonged to her, ' that
you will not bring the dear lad all this long

way for *nothing*. You see the fare is of some consequence to a poor Government clerk.'

Mary strove to look ignorant of the widow's meaning, but her blushes belied her; indeed, considering what the burthen of Charley's daily letters had been for some time past, it was difficult to ignore it. She preferred, however, to answer the latter part of Mrs. Sotheran's speech instead of the former.

'I don't see why Charley should consider the fare,' she said evasively. 'Mr. Rennie was telling me in his very last letter something about the dividends being due this month that would make him quite a Crœsus.'

'Charley's dividends! Why, my dear Mary, do you suppose that Charley would ever take or touch one shilling of *that* money? It must be paid to him, I suppose, since it was left to him, because poor Hilda dared not leave it to you directly. But if you think that, except as your husband, he will ever reap any benefit from it, you do not know him as his mother does.'

' I never heard of such a thing,' said Mary.
' The idea of his not taking his own money ! '

' My dear, it is not his own. As Mr. Rennie
will tell you, all these matters depend upon the
intentions of the testator, and there is no question in this case about them. Indeed, as poor
Charley writes to me, though he is too delicate-
minded to urge that plea with you, every day
you delay your marriage you are flying in the
face of your poor grandmother's wishes.'

' But she has been dead such a little while,'
sighed Mary.

'If she had had her will, you would have
been married while she was yet alive ; and I
am sure that it would distress her—if a saint in
heaven can be touched by trouble—to think
that the happiness of her dear ones is being
postponed for her sake. It is, at the best, a
very conventional view of duty, Mary.'

I am afraid these sentiments had not
originated in the widow's breast, but had been
cunningly suggested to her by another, with the
request that she should adopt them as her own.

'Well. if *you* think so, Mrs. Sotheran,' admitted Mary. 'I am sure it cannot be wrong; and if Charley is so silly as to deny himself. unless I share them, the comforts which I am sure my dear grandmother meant him to enjoy, why——'

'Just so,' put in Mrs. Sotheran, her wits sharpened by maternal love; 'it would, as you were about to say. be acting very selfishly to Charley, and even a little like the dog in the manger.'

So it was not 'for nothing' that Charley came down at midsummer; only it was agreed that since. if it happened at Letcombe Dottrell, it would put Mr. Wells, the vicar, in an embarrassing position as regarded his patron, the wedding—in spite of the indignant protest of Lady Orr. who wrote, 'If I were in your place, my dear, I would be married under your grandfather's nose '—took place in London. It was done in the quietest way; but Mr. Rennie, who gave the bride away, took very good care that the world should know all about it. The announcement of the auspicious event not only set forth Mary's parentage in a perspicuous manner, but added (just as though he had had a title, in which case, even if he is but a knight, one's grandfather always puts in an appearance), 'and granddaughter of Beryl Peyton, of Letcombe Hall.' After which assertion of the bride's aristocratic lineage, the happy pair went prudently into lodgings.

The money that good Mrs. Peyton had left them did not produce 'an income to marry upon' in the eyes of fashion, but then Charley and Mary (as I hope we have made sufficiently clear) were not fashionable people. They would have been very happy could they have seen more of one another, but the Probate Office took up most of Charley's day, and, though she never told him so, Mary had rather a weary time of it in his absence. There is no place, it is well known, like home, but there is also no place so little like home as London lodgings. Notwithstanding which there were many palatial residences, and especially a certain one in Park Lane, where there was not one tenth of the wedded happiness enjoyed by this unambitious young couple.

CHAPTER LIII.

THE DISPUTED WILL.

It was Charley's habit at breakfast time (no
doubt engendered by official duties, which
comprehend, I have noticed, a good deal of
casual newspaper-reading) to skim over a
penny paper. One morning he found some
news in it of more than public interest—it was
a long obituary, headed ' Death of Mr. Beryl
Peyton, the philanthropist.'

The epithet would have made some men's
lips curl had they stood in Charley's place, but
he had never nourished a bitter thought
against the old man. He had always dis-
couraged the suggestion that Mr. Peyton was
behaving in an unnatural manner, and had
shown himself to be Mary's enemy. He held

that Beryl Peyton's case was an exceptional one, where nature had been 'expelled with a pitchfork' from what was otherwise a noble heart, and that he was nobody's enemy but his own. It was a subject on which he did not talk much to his wife; he understood that her reverence for her mother's memory, her indignation on her grandmother's account, and the neglect with which she herself had been treated in her youth, caused her to take severer views of her grandfather. But now that the man was beyond man's judgment, he knew her gentle heart would have no room in it for any but charitable thoughts.

'My darling,' he said, 'your grandfather is dead.'

She put down her tea-cup, rose, and, walking to the window, stood there a moment or two, looking out into the street, but seeing nothing.

'God help him and forgive us all,' she presently answered.

'Amen,' said Charley. 'The poor old

fellow was found dead in his bed yesterday morning. The paper says he is to be buried at Lorton.'

'In the cathedral?'

'Yes.'

'That was not his wish; he enjoined upon me, if he omitted to leave any instructions to that effect, that I was to state that he wished to be buried under Dottrell Knob.'

'How strange! The writer of the obituary, however, can of course know nothing about such matters yet. He speaks of the cathedral as being the proper place for a man of such public mark and usefulness in his locality to lie.'

Nothing more was said; and Charley went his way, taking a somewhat graver farewell of his young wife than usual.

His fellow-clerks at the office were full of the news. 'The old fellow will not surely carry his resentment beyond the grave, Sotheran,' said one. 'He will cut you off at worst with twenty thou. or so.'

'What a day it will be for you when his will comes in for proof, my lad!' said another. 'You will be the first man I ever knew with a million of money.'

These congratulations were not welcome to Charley—not that he felt, or could be expected to feel, much personal regret at what had happened, but they were distasteful to him on his wife's account, into whose mind no thought of material advantage from her grandfather's death had ever entered.

The question 'Who will be Beryl Peyton's heir?' however, was one that excited much curiosity, and the husband of his only relative was naturally a subject for speculation.

On the third day Mr. Rennie looked in upon the young couple, with a lugubrious face, which to Mary seemed sufficiently accounted for by the circumstances.

She spoke to him about her grandfather, and, avoiding all unpleasant topics, reminded him of what he had said of him on the occasion of Mrs. Peyton's funeral; how that no man had taken more delight in making others happy, or done more good without a thought of self.

'That is quite true,' said the lawyer, gravely; 'but when wronged (as though he felt that he of all men least deserved to be so), he resented it with extreme bitterness and obstinacy. I am sorry to say, my dear Mrs. Sotheran, that he nourished that resentment in your case to the last.'

'I am sorry too,' she gently said.

What she meant was that she was sorry upon his account, not on her own; but the other mistook her, imagining her quietness of tone to signify resignation to pecuniary loss.

· Just so,' he answered, 'you are sorry, but not surprised. I confess that I had hoped he would not utterly have forgotten the claims of his own flesh and blood. But I regret to say it is so. I have seen Macalister. There are a great many legacies, but none to those who had most right to expect them. He has made Edgar Dornay his heir.'

'He might have made a worse,' said Charley, generously.

'And also a better,' sighed the lawyer. 'I can only say I did my best for you.'

Mary gave him a grateful smile, and Charley wrung his hand.

'That is the one thing we shall think of concerning this matter, Mr. Rennie,' he said—'your great kindness. Of disappointment there is nothing, for there was no expectation. You have no idea how happy we are.'

Being a bachelor, it is probable he had not. But 'It does not matter now' was what was in the lawyer's thoughts, 'but when the children come, and this contented little firm becomes an unlimited company, a few thousands of Beryl Peyton's money would come in extremely handy.'

Then they fell to talking about the funeral, which Mary thought her husband ought to attend.

'Very good,' said Charley. 'I am not fond of funerals, but it is to Beryl Peyton that

I owe you, my darling, and therefore I shall go.'

'I would not, if I were you,' said the lawyer, drily. 'You can do him no good ; and, as no one believes in gratitude, your presence will only be set down to expectancy.'

'That's a very hateful notion,' observed Charley.

'Yes, but I have noticed that many people's notions are hateful. If you take my advice, you will make no sign in this matter.'

This was agreed to, and then Charley inquired whether Mr. Peyton had left any particular orders as to his interment : on Mr. Rennie's replying that he had not done so, he told him what the deceased had said to Mary on that subject. The lawyer seemed rather struck with it.

'He wanted to be buried under the Knob, did he? I wish he *had* left that memorandum behind him.'

'But ought not Mary to speak?'

'Certainly not. The motive would be misconstrued.'

'Motive? What motive?'

'Good heavens! what a pair of turtle-doves you are! Without the wisdom of the serpent you might surely have guessed that such a will, made by such a man, is sure to be disputed. Do you suppose Edgar Dornay will become the richest man in England without a fight for it? Beryl Peyton has made half a dozen other heirs, to my knowledge. They 'll dispute his last testament, of course.'

'Upon what ground?'

'Ground? As if we lawyers, like a mere Archimedes, could move nothing without ground! But in this case there are acres of it. Undue influence — madness, the latter especially. That is why you must say nothing about his wanting to be buried under Dottrell Knob—an intention on the part of the testator which certainly points that way. People would say you wanted to prove him mad.'

'And if we did, how could that benefit us?'

inquired Charley. 'If the last will was shown to be invalid, then the last but one would hold good; would it not?'

'I had forgotten you were in the Probate Office,' said the lawyer, drily. 'Still, I advise you to say nothing about the Knob.'

At the end of the week came the funeral—an affair of great pomp and magnificence. It was a dull time in the journalistic world, and therefore the papers were full of it. Reporters described the scene, and delicately implied that they were personally moved by it: 'Who could hear that noble anthem, "When the ear heard him then it blessed him," peal over the remains of such a man without,' &c. It really was, however, an affecting scene. There were more genuine tears at Beryl Peyton's grave than were ever shed over that of prince or warrior. Men were there whom he had raised up from death—the death of indigence and despair—to a life of honesty and content; women whom he had saved from terrible temptations; orphans to whom he had been a generous father. There was scarcely any class of his fellow-creatures which did not comprise a witness to his virtues. It was stated that Mr. Edgar Dornay, the heir to the deceased's great estates, and whose skill and taste had so long been known in artistic circles, was designing a magnificent monument to his memory which would be intrusted to the most eminent of modern sculptors. ' But,' added the composer of the paragraph, with less of originality than truth, ' Beryl Peyton needs no monument : his work survives him and testifies to his worth.'

Then when Eulogy, which has a short breath, was exhausted, Slander took up the tale. Mr. Beryl Peyton had done some liberal things, no doubt, but the catalogue of his vice was endless, and also very curious. He had himself dragged iniquity with a cart-rope, but in his son's case would not pardon a peccadillo. Public sympathy for his granddaughter took the more agreeable, because the more exciting, shape of indignation against the stranger he had made his heir. Mary Sotheran, as we know, was excluded by a special clause from deriving any possible benefit from her grandfather's will: if Edgar Dornay should attempt to right matters ever so slightly, he lost all. But the world at large knew nothing of that, or credited nothing, and the sensitive Edgar was the mark for ten thousand stings. The golden salve of a million of money could not cure them. And he had not got the money. The will gave it him. but. as Mr. Rennie had predicted, more than one person—'parties'—disputed the will.

This is not the place to describe the great Beryl Peyton will case, the *cause célèbre* of the Court of Probate. It was said of the deceased, as can be said of few rich men, that in his lifetime he had neither been ostentatious nor litigious, had not done much for either the newspapers or the lawyers; but he made it up to them after his demise. The details of the trial took the place of the proceedings in Parliament, which fortunately (for the journals) was not sitting; and the gentlemen of the long robe settled down upon his remains—that is, upon what he had left behind him—like crows upon an elm-top. He had, it seemed, instructed Mr. Macalister to destroy his fine collection of wills, with two exceptions: the one, of course, under which Mr. Edgar Dornay claimed to succeed to the property, and a previous one, executed but a few months before, by which Messrs. Marks and Nayler came in for a considerable cantle. The view of these philosophers, supported by an enterprising firm of solicitors who took up their case from motives of benevolence, and because they thought it a very good one, was first that Mr. Edgar Dornay had exercised undue influence over the deceased, especially in the few weeks preceding his death, when, indeed, he had been paramount at the Hall; and, secondly, that Mr. Beryl Peyton had, before executing his last testament, become *non compos mentis.* He had certainly done some very curious things. Gone to church, for example, on a week day when there was no service, and, after passing a couple of hours in his pew alone, expressed himself as more gratified with his experience there than he had ever been in his life; he had gravely suggested that Dr. Bilde should write 'An Autobiography of a Vivisectionist' for the 'Animal World,' the organ of the Society for the Prevention of Cruelty to Animals; and he had made proposals in writing for the bringing out of one Japhet Marcom, a deaf mute, as a public singer.

These facts were dilated upon by no less than five counsel, and denied upon Mr. Edgar Dornay's behalf by five others instructed by Mr. Macalister. They were not true, they argued; and if they were true, so far from being symptomatic of alienation of mind, argued a high degree of intelligence. As to that solitary church-going, was not no sermon (to the ear of criticism) often to be preferred even to a short one? As to the 'Animal World,' was not the narrative of a life steeped in crime often found to be more deterrent than goody-goody anecdotes were found conducive to good conduct?

As to the suggestion of bringing out the deaf mute at Covent Garden, had not a street organ without a barrel turned out a great success within the memory of an intelligent jury? Or, taking another view, was it not certain that three fourths of the people who went to the opera in reality were bored with the singing? and what was more natural than to suppose that Beryl Peyton, whose life-long object had been to promote the happiness of the greatest number, should have had this also in view in his last testament?

What the advocates on Mr. Edgar Dornay's side, however, most dwelt upon, was the eccentricity of conduct which had marked the whole course of the deceased's existence.

'Good heavens!' cried the leading counsel, with emotion, ' why, who ever heard out of a story book of any other man going about doing good on the same extensive scale without taking indirect but efficient measures to have it properly reported in the public press? Of what other man in a like position was it recorded that, with his enormous local influence, he had never exerted it for his own benefit, but had plodded on (if he might use the expression) on his 50,000*l.* a year, without asking the Government for so much as a baronetcy? What other man had exercised patronage and munificence on such a scale, and never looked for his *quid pro quo* in the way of flattery or even subservience? Why, all this is so contrary to human experience—I had almost said, gentlemen of the jury, to human nature, that it might well have aroused the suspicion—if the case were another man's—of his having been stark staring mad! Yet who of all the subjects of his benevolence, and doubtless often undeserved benevolence, has ever suggested that Mr. Beryl Peyton was out of his mind? It is true, his son made such an allegation—that son of whom, remembering the beautiful injunction of the Latin poet, *de mortuis nil nisi bonum*, I will say nothing—but why did he do it? For the same reason that the suggestion is made now : in order to gratify his greed at the expense of justice. If eccentricity is madness, then indeed my client is in evil case, but in no worse case than our opponents. Witnesses will be produced before you who will testify to many acts, anterior to the will of the 10th of September last, on which my learned friends on the other side have taken their stand, fully as unusual and eccentric, but doubtless quite as easy of explanation, as those committed during the last months or weeks of the deceased's existence.'

Whereupon Mr. Reuben Burzon was produced, with such an unvarnished tale of Mr. Beryl Peyton's *protégés*—acrobats, wild beast tamers, and repentant thieves—as made the hair of all the jury save one (who had none) fairly stand on end with astonishment; also a South American gentleman (imported at an immense expense) whom the late Mr. Beryl Peyton had thrown into a dock and left to drown apparently for no particular reason; also certain waiters who had seen the deceased dining alone at a table laid for twelve persons, and heard him returning thanks for his health being drunk by nobody, in a most appropriate speech.

To read all this for week after week was very painful to poor Mary, though at the same time it afforded her some comfort; for, as Charley observed with characteristic naturalness, 'If your grandfather was so queer as this, my dear, in his ordinary relations in life, what wonder is it that he was queer to his blood relations? If I were you, I wouldn't think anything more about it—I wouldn't, really. It is clear to me that he was touched in his head; and I only hope' (here he kissed her, and winked with a significant slyness which brought the colour to her cheeks) 'that that sort of thing is not going to be hereditary.'

Mr. Rennie also read the case with mingled feelings: it was wormwood to him that Mr. Macalister should have the conduct of it, but very pleasant to reflect that he was not doing it well. It was the lawyer's private opinion that Mr. Edgar Dornay's counsel were overdoing the eccentricity argument and getting on rather dangerous ground for all parties.

The sympathies of the young couple could hardly be said to be enlisted on either side, though they would have certainly preferred to see Edgar Dornay victorious than the two philosophers; and when the evidence was over they probably took less interest in the decision than many persons who were wholly unconnected with the matter.

CHAPTER LIV.

THE VERDICT.

IT was December, and Mrs. Sotheran had been persuaded with little difficulty to come up from Letcombe Dottrell to pass Christmas with her young people. The emptiness of the great house made the neighbourhood dull, and the lonely widow more *triste* than ever; and the thought of returning home when the Hall should have found an owner was very disagreeable to her, since in no case would she have a friend in her neighbour. Though she had never had very cheerful matters to discourse about with Mrs. Peyton, she missed her companionship very much. There was even some talk of Mrs. Sotheran coming to live with the young couple, which, however, that lady, who was as wise in some matters as she was simple in others, was loth to do. On the other hand, a partnership of income would enable her son to take some modest home of his own a little way out of London, which in view of a certain contingency—the arrival of a little stranger—would be more convenient than the living in lodgings. They were discussing the *pros* and *cons* of this project after dinner, when they heard the visitors' bell ring: the wheels of his chariot they had not heard, for there was a deep snow on the ground, and when he entered he was hardly recognisable by reason of his cloaks and 'wraps.' As no one, however, took such care of himself (externally) as Mr. Rennie, they identified him at once.

' Oh, this *is* good of you !' said Mary. ' Why, I thought you said the other day you had to go into the country, and would not be able to see us again till the New Year ? '

' Well, yes ; but the fact is, something has occurred to defer my visit, and I thought I'd just look in to—to wish you a merry Christmas.'

He filled his glass, and at his request they all did the like. It was no conventional ' compliment of the season ' (a phrase I detest above all others), but an interchange of the heartiest good wishes.

It would have been difficult to find four people, so very different in character, who respected one another more.

' By-the-by, I 've got a bit of news for you : the verdict's out.'

' They 've been time enough about it,' observed Charley, composedly. ' The jury were left deliberating at twelve o'clock.'

' Well, you see it was a big case. Your friends the philosophers have lost it.'

' I am deuced glad of it,' said Charley frankly.

' I am afraid they cannot afford to lose it,' murmured Mary, pityingly. ' Will not the expenses be very heavy ? '

' The costs are to be paid out of the estate.'

' Come, that 's very satisfactory. I may now

confess,' said Mary, ' that I am glad Mr. Dornay has beaten them.'

' Naturally; he is an old friend,' said the lawyer, winking with an unexampled slyness at Charley. ' Still, if the others had won, they might have given the " rightful heir " a douceur of ten thousand pounds or so in the way of compensation, whereas Dornay is bound by the will from doing so. It was only the other day that you were saying to me, Charley, how very handy ten thousand pounds would come in.'

' I never spoke so disrespectfully of any such sum,' said Charley, laughing, but with the colour in his cheeks, and a little displeased that his wife should hear of a wish that might suggest discontent in him. ' I said that ten thousand pounds seemed to me just the perfection of a fortune, and that as to anything more I should not know what to do with it.'

' Then if you were left with a million of money, what would you do with the nine hundred and ninety thousand pounds?'

' But you see I have not been left it.'

'No, but your wife has been!'

It was not Mr. Rennie's way to joke upon business matters, but for the moment they all thought him influenced by the associations of the season—that he was slightly pantomimic. There was a pause, and three forced smiles.

'I am incorrect in saying that Mrs. Charles Sotheran has been left this great fortune,' continued the lawyer, gravely, 'except so far as the law can be said to leave it. That fellow Macalister (the solicitor ignored the five counsel) has been hoist with his own petard. The jury have decided that Mr. Beryl Peyton was not in a condition to manage his own affairs or dispose of his property anterior to the 18th of September last, whereby both his last testaments are rendered null and void. The whole property consequently reverts to Mr. Peyton's next of kin. He used to say that the proverb "Blood is thicker than water" was all rubbish, but in the eye of the law, I am glad to say, the old saw holds good. Riches are deceitful, but still I must needs congratulate you, Mrs. Charles

Sotheran, on being one of the wealthiest women in England.'

It would be a proof of imagination in a man of letters, indeed, if he could conceive the feeling of an individual who unexpectedly finds himself possessed of a million of money. I can assert with confidence, however, that Mary Sotheran was more astonished than gratified. A sense of responsibility hung like a great cloud over the brilliant future thus presented to her, and dulled its brightness; its contrast with her past was too tremendous. She was overwhelmed with the burthen to which she had not been born.

'It is like a terrible fairy tale,' she murmured: ' I cannot grasp it as a reality.'

' Well, I suppose we shall not now live in lodgings, *that's* certain,' observed Charley, with the air of a man who has found firm ground, if there was but a foot of it.

' Heaven have mercy on us!' ejaculated the poor little widow. ' Heaven have mercy on us!' at intervals, like minute guns. She was so accustomed to calamities that this amazing prosperity had for her something of the nature of a final catastrophe.

In a month's time, however, they were all living at Letcombe Hall, a ' happy family ' of a very different kind from that which had formerly inhabited it. Charley threw up his clerkship in the Probate Office without a struggle; but it was averred by his former superiors (after his elevation) that they had never known a young official of such promise, and that the country had sustained a severe loss in his retirement from the public service.

If I forget to mention any one of those persons who had shown kindness to Mary Marvon in her need, we may be sure that Mrs. Charles Sotheran did not forget them. The whole of the old household at the Hall, except the valet (who received the pension his late master had intended for him), were retained; and if Japhet Marcom did not sing for joy, it was for a reason with which we are acquainted: he had good cause to do so.

Every intention of the deceased with respect to legacies was carried out to the letter. Even the two philosophers, though Mary had small cause to 'remember' them in the douceur sense, were not forgotten, nor did Dr. Bilde lose his stipulated honorarium for professional attendance on his late patron, though the codicil that had given it to him was, of course, waste-paper like the rest. The whole Happy Family were, in short, made at least as happy as they deserved to be. Mr. Rennie thought his client's conduct very Quixotic, but then, 'what else was to be expected in a descendant of Beryl Peyton's?'

This liberality was nevertheless in some cases very far from giving satisfaction to its recipients. Mr. Marks published a pamphlet entitled 'The Beggar on Horseback Riding Sideways,' designed to lampoon his benefactress; but, unable to eliminate from the composition the 'categories' and the 'noumenons,' only about half a dozen folks understood what he was driving at, and, being themselves metaphysicians, they were unable to explain it to other people.

Mr. Nayler, whose circle of flesh-and-blood acquaintances had become, since his patron's death, extremely limited, confined himself to observing, with much bitterness, that he could hardly have imagined any one so utterly false and hollow as Mrs. Charles Sotheran, even if it had fallen to his lot to *make* a presentment; a remark which the public (who conceived his head to have been turned by the late trial) imagined to be a reference to some grand jury.

One of the first persons to whom Mary's thoughts reverted, so soon as she found herself endowed, as by a fairy wand, with the power of doing good, was Mr. Tidman. That worthy man is now the proprietor of one of the finest hotels on the South Coast, that locality having been chosen on account of the supposed delicacy of his lady, who is more ethereal than ever, and occupies the best apartments on the first floor, as though she were a guest, and had even less to do with the management of the establishment than she really has. This improvement of position only recalls more vividly the memory of better days, and the associations in connection with the late Sir Anthony Blenkinhouse, Baronet, of the Manor, Slopton, over which she still sheds copious tears. Her husband superintends all matters of importance with great diligence and sagacity, and only regrets he has no time for everything. When he has half an hour of leisure he locks himself in his private parlour, and it is whispered (though he takes the precaution to put paper in the keyhole) gives himself up to details—takes off his coat, and with the old superfluous energy transforms the table into a mirror.

Miss Julia Blithers, although in no need of pecuniary assistance, sent her warmest congratulations to Mary upon her good fortune. ' My book,' she wrote, in the highest spirits, ' is coming out at last. You will gather from this fact that poor dear Sarah is dead. I understand that you are acquainted with Mr. Dornay the poet.   If you can get me his autograph you will be conferring on me a great obligation, but if not, I dare say I can procure it '—which I have no sort of doubt she did.

Edgar, deprived of his million, has taken quite a high place among our Bards of Despondency, and drawn tears from a thousand eyes, or, to speak less vaguely (for his public is limited), from two hundred and fifty pairs of them.

Mr. Ralph Dornay has not, I regret to say, turned out altogether as we could have wished, but his wife finds him less unendurable : the fact is, they are separated.   He has been induced, thanks to Mr. Rennie's good offices, to retire from Park Lane upon a very handsome pension.

Lady Orr once remarked, in speaking of him to Mary, ' Your grandfather, my dear, used to say that there was nothing so difficult to extricate oneself from as the tie of blood ; but there he made a great mistake—there 's matrimony.'

Notwithstanding which assertion of her ladyship, Mr. Rennie maintains that if anything should happen to Ralph Dornay, he should not be the least surprised to receive his widow's instructions for another 'settlement.' 'One talks of a " marrying man," ' he says, 'but after an experience or two, *he* learns to know better : a marrying woman nothing can cure.'

After a silence of a quarter of a century, the great walled garden at Letcombe Hall echoes once more to children's laughter. If Mrs. Peyton from her abode in heaven is permitted to listen to it, it is a music we may be sure that will not mar for her the angel choir, nor will it now jar upon her husband's ear, who, as I trust, is now inhabiting the same mansion in the skies. We vanish away, it is true, like a breath, but on the glass of memory some linger a little longer than others. Of all the persons described in this little life-drama, Beryl Peyton will live longest in human remembrance, and in my poor judgment, with all his faults, will deserve to live.

THE END.